CROWN PRINCE'S CHOSEN BRIDE

BY

KANDY SHEPHERD

All rights reserved including the right of reproduction
in whole or in part in any form. This edition is published
by arrangement with Harlequin Books S.A.

This is a work of fiction. Names, characters, places,
locations and incidents are purely fictional and bear
no relationship to any real life individuals, living or
dead, or to any actual places, business establishments,
locations, events or incidents. Any resemblance is entirely
coincidental.

This book is sold subject to the condition that it shall not,
by way of trade or otherwise, be lent, resold, hired out
or otherwise circulated without the prior consent of the
publisher in any form of binding or cover other than that
in which it is published and without a similar condition
including this condition being imposed on the subsequent
purchaser.

® and TM are trademarks owned and used by the
trademark owner and/or its licensee. Trademarks
marked with ® are registered with the United Kingdom
Patent Office and/or the Office for Harmonisation in the
Internal Market and in other countries.

First published in Great Britain 2016
By Mills & Boon, an imprint of HarperCollins*Publishers*
1 London Bridge Street, London, SE1 9GF

Large Print edition 2016

© 2016 Kandy Shepherd 7/16

ISBN: 978-0-263-26214-8

Our policy is to use papers that are natural, renewable
and recyclable products and made from wood grown
in sustainable forests. The logging and manufacturing
processes conform to the legal environmental regulations
of the country of origin.

Printed and bound in Great Britain
by CPI Antony Rowe, Chippenham, Wiltshire

To Cathleen Ross,
in gratitude for your friendship!

CHAPTER ONE

USING AN OLD-FASHIONED wooden spoon and her favourite vintage-style ceramic bowl, Gemma Harper beat the batter for the cake she was baking to mark the end of her six months' self-imposed exile from dating.

Fittingly, the cake was a mixture of sweet and sour—a rich white chocolate mud cake, flavoured with the sharp contrast of lemon and lime. For Gemma, the six months had been sweet with the absence of relationship angst and tempered by sour moments of loneliness. But she'd come out of it stronger, wiser, determined to break the cycle of choosing the wrong type of man. *The heartbreaking type.*

From now on things would be different, she reminded herself as she gave the batter a particularly vigorous stir. She would not let a handsome face and a set of broad shoulders blind her to character flaws that spelled ultimate doom to happiness. She would curb the impulsiveness that had

seen her diving headlong into relationships because she thought she was in love with someone
she, in fact, did not really know.

And she was going to be much, *much* tougher.
Less forgiving. No more giving 'one last chance'
and then another to a cheating, lying heartbreaker,
unworthy of her, whose false promises she'd believed.

She was twenty-eight and she wanted to get
married and have kids before too many more
years sped by.

'No more Ms Bad Judge of Men,' she said out
loud.

It was okay to talk to herself. She was alone in
the large industrial kitchen at the converted ware-
house in inner-city Alexandria, the Sydney suburb that was headquarters to her successful party
planning business. Party Queens belonged to her
and to her two business partners, Andie New-
man and Eliza Dunne. The food was Gemma's
domain, Andie was the creative genius and Eliza
the business brain.

After several years working as a chef and then
as a food editor on magazines, in Party Queens
Gemma had found her dream job. Going into
partnership with Andie and Eliza was the best

decision she'd ever made. And throwing herself headlong into work had been the best thing she could have done to keep her mind off men. She would do anything to keep this business thriving.

Gemma poured the batter into a high, round pan and carefully placed it into a slow oven, where it would cook for one and a half hours. Then she would cover it with coconut frosting and garnish it with fine curls of candied lemon and lime peel. Not only would the cake be a treat for her and her partners to share this afternoon, in celebration of the end of her man-free six months, it was also a trial run for a client's wedding cake.

Carefully, she settled the cake in the centre of the oven and gently closed the oven door.

She turned back to face the island countertop, to find she was no longer alone. A tall, broad-shouldered man stood just inside the door. She gasped, and her hand—encased in a hot-pink oven mitt—went to her heart.

'Who are you and how the heck did you get in here?' she asked, her voice high with sudden panic.

Even through her shock she registered that the intruder was very handsome, with a lean face and light brown hair. *Just her type.* No. *No longer her type*—not after six months of talking herself out of that kind of very good-looking man. Especially if he was a burglar—or worse.

She snatched up a wooden spoon in self-defence. Drips of cake batter slid down her arm, but she scarcely noticed.

The man put up his hands as if to ward off her spoon. 'Tristan Marco. I have a meeting this morning with Eliza Dunne. She called to tell me she was caught in traffic and gave me the pass code for the door.'

The stranger seemed about her age and spoke with a posh English accent laced with a trace of something else. Something she couldn't quite place. French? German? He didn't look Australian. Something about his biscuit-coloured linen trousers, fine cream cotton shirt and stylish shoes seemed sartorially European.

'You can put down your weapon,' he said, amusement rippling through his voice.

Gemma blushed as she lowered the wooden spoon. What good would a spoon have been against a man taller than six foot? She took a deep breath in an attempt to get her heart rate back to somewhere near normal. 'You gave me quite a shock, walking in on me like that. Why didn't you press the buzzer?'

He walked further into the room so he stood opposite the island counter that separated them. This close she noticed vivid blue eyes framed by dark brows, smooth olive skin, perfect teeth.

'I'm sorry to have frightened you,' he said in that intriguing accent and with an expressive shrug of his broad shoulders. 'Ms Dunne did not tell me anyone else would be here.'

Gemma took off her oven mitts, used one to surreptitiously wipe the batter dribbles from her arm and placed them on the countertop.

'I wasn't frightened. It's just that I'm on my own here and—' *now wasn't* that *a dumb thing to say to a stranger?* '—Eliza will be here very soon.'

'Yes, she said she would not be long,' he said. His smile was both charming and reassuring. 'I'm looking forward to meeting her. We have only spoken on the phone.'

He was gorgeous. Gemma refused to let the dangerous little fluttering of awareness take hold. She had just spent six months talking herself out of any kind of instant attraction. She was not going to make those old mistakes again.

'Can I help you in the meantime?' Gemma

asked. 'I'm Gemma Harper—one of Eliza's business partners.'

To be polite, she moved around the countertop to be nearer to him. Realising she was still in her white chef's apron, she went to untie it, then stopped. Might that look as if she was *undressing* in front of this stranger?

She gave herself a mental shake. *Of course it wouldn't.* Had six months without a date made her start thinking like an adolescent? Still, there was no real need to take the apron off.

She offered him her hand in a businesslike gesture that she hoped negated the pink oven mitts and the wielding of the wooden spoon. He took it in his own firm, warm grip for just the right amount of time.

'So you are also a Party Queen?' he asked. The hint of a smile lifted the corners of his mouth.

'Yes, I'm the food director,' she said, wishing not for the first time that they had chosen a more staid name for the business. It had all started as a bit of a lark, but now, eighteen months after they had launched, they were one of the most popular and successful party planning businesses in Sydney. And still being teased about being Party Queens.

'Did you…did you want to see Eliza about booking a party?' she asked cautiously. To her knowledge, the steadfastly single Eliza wasn't dating anyone. But his visit to their headquarters might be personal. Lucky Eliza, if that was the case.

'Yes, I've been planning a reception with her.'

'A reception? You mean a wedding reception?'

The good ones were always taken. She banished the flickering disappointment the thought aroused. This guy was a stranger and a client. His marital status should be of no concern to her. Yet she had to admit there was something about him she found very attractive beyond the obvious appeal of his good looks. Perhaps because he seemed somehow…different.

'No. Not a wedding.' His face seemed to darken. 'When I get married, it will not be *me* arranging the festivities.'

Of course it wouldn't. In her experience it was always the bride. It sometimes took the grooms a while to realise that.

'So, if not a wedding reception, what kind of reception?'

'Perhaps "reception" is not the right word. My English…' He shrugged again.

She did like broad shoulders on a man.

'Your English sounds perfect to me,' she said, her curiosity aroused. 'Do you mean a business reception?'

'Yes and no. I have been speaking to Eliza about holding a party for me to meet Australians connected by business to my family. It is to be held on Friday evening.'

It clicked. 'Of course!' she exclaimed. 'The cocktail party at the Parkview Hotel on Friday night.' It was now Monday, and everything was on track for the upscale event.

'That is correct,' he said.

'I manage the food aspect of our business. We're using the hotel's excellent catering team. I've worked with them on devising the menu. I think you'll be very happy with the food.'

'It all looked in order to me,' he said. 'I believe I am in capable hands.'

Everything fell into place. Tristan Marco was their mystery client. Mysterious because his event had been organised from a distance, by phone and email, in a hurry, and by someone for whom Eliza had been unable to check credit details. The client had solved that problem by paying the entire quoted price upfront. A very substantial price for a no-expenses-spared party at a high-end venue.

She, Eliza and Andie had spent quite some time speculating on what the client would be like.

'You are in the best possible hands with our company,' she reassured him.

He looked at her intently, his blue eyes narrowed. 'Did I speak with you?' he said. 'I am sure I would have remembered your voice.'

She certainly would have remembered *his.*

Gemma shook her head. 'Eliza is our business director. She does most of our client liaison. You are not what we—' She clapped her hand to her mouth. *Put a zip on it, Gemma.*

'Not what you what?' he asked with a quizzical expression.

'Not…not what we expected,' she said. Her voice trailed away, and she looked down in the direction of his well-polished Italian shoes.

'What *did* you expect?'

She sighed and met his gaze full on. There was no getting out of this. She really needed to curb her tendency to blurt things out without thinking. That was why she worked with the food and Eliza and Andie with the clients.

'Well, we expected someone older. Someone not so tall. Someone heavier. Someone perhaps even…bald. With a twirling black moustache.

Maybe…maybe someone like Hercule Poirot. You know…the detective in the Agatha Christie movies?'

Someone not so devastatingly handsome.

Thank heaven, he laughed. 'So are you disappointed in what you see?' He stood, arms outspread, as if welcoming her inspection.

Gemma felt suddenly breathless at the intensity of his gaze, at her compulsion to take up his unspoken offer to admire his tall, obviously well-muscled body, his lean, handsome face with those incredibly blue eyes, the full sensual mouth with the top lip slightly narrower then the lower, the way his short brown hair kicked up at the front in a cowlick.

'Not at all,' she said, scarcely able to choke out the words. *Disappointed was* not *the word that sprang to mind.*

'I am glad to hear that,' he said very seriously, his gaze not leaving hers. 'You did not know me, but I knew *exactly* what to expect from Party Queens.'

'You…you did?' she stuttered.

'Party Queens was recommended to me by my friend Jake Marlowe. He told me that each of the three partners was beautiful, talented and very smart.'

'He…he did?' she said, her vocabulary seeming to have escaped her.

Billionaire Jake Marlowe was the business partner of Andie's husband, Dominic. He'd been best man at their wedding two Christmases ago. Who knew he'd taken such an interest in them?

'On the basis of my meeting with you, I can see Jake did not mislead me,' Tristan said.

His formal way of speaking and his charming smile made the compliment sound sincere when it might have sounded sleazy. *Had he even made a slight bow as he spoke?*

She willed herself not to blush again but without success. 'Thank you,' was all she could manage to say.

'Jake spoke very highly of your business,' Tristan said. 'He told me there was no better party-planning company in Sydney.'

'That was kind of him. It's always gratifying to get such good feedback.'

'I did not even talk with another company,' Tristan said with that charming smile.

'Wow! I mean…that's wonderful. I…we're flattered. We won't let you down, I promise you. The hotel is a perfect venue. It overlooks Hyde Park, it's high end, elegant and it prides itself on its exemplary service. I don't think I've ever seen so much marble and glamour in one place.'

She knew she was speaking too fast, but she couldn't seem to help it.

'Yes. The first thing I did was inspect it when I arrived in Sydney. You chose well.' He paused. 'I myself would prefer something more informal, but protocol dictates the event must be formal.'

'The protocol of your family business?' she asked, not quite sure she'd got it right.

He nodded. 'That is correct. It must be upheld even when I am in another country.'

'You're a visitor to Australia?' Another piece of the puzzle fell into place. The phone calls had all come from Queensland, the state to the north of New South Wales. Where Jake Marlowe lived, she now realised.

'Yes,' he said.

She still couldn't place the accent, and it annoyed her. Gemma had studied French, German and Italian—not that she'd had much chance to practise them—and thought she had a good ear.

'What kind of business does your family run?' she asked.

That was another thing the Party Queens had wondered about as they'd discussed their mystery client. *He was still a mystery.*

Tristan was still too bemused by the vision of this cute redhead wearing bright pink oven mitts and wielding a wooden spoon as a weapon to think straight. He had to consider his reply and try not to be distracted by the smear of flour down her right cheek that seemed to point to her beautiful full mouth. While he'd been speaking with her, he'd had to fight the urge to lean across and gently wipe it off.

Should he tell her the truth? Or give the same evasive replies he'd given to others during his incognito trip to Sydney? He'd been here four days, and no one had recognised him…

Visiting Australia had been on his list to do before he turned thirty and had to return home to step up his involvement in 'the business'. He'd spent some time in Queensland with Jake. But for the past few days in Sydney, he had enjoyed his anonymity, relished being just Tristan. No expectations. No explanations. Just a guy nearing thirty, being himself, being independent, having fun. It was a novelty for him to be an everyday guy. Even when he'd been at university in England, the other students had soon sussed him out.

He would have to tell Party Queens the truth about himself and the nature of his reception sooner or later, though. *Let it be later.*

Gemma Harper was lovely—really lovely—with her deep auburn hair, heart-shaped face and the shapely curves that the professional-looking white apron did nothing to disguise. He wanted to enjoy talking with her still cloaked in the anonymity of being just plain Tristan. When she found out his true identity, her attitude would change. It always did.

'Finance. Trade. That kind of thing,' he replied.

'I see,' she said.

He could tell by the slight downturn of her mouth that although she'd made the right polite response, she found his family business dull. More the domain of the portly, bald gentleman she'd imagined him to be. Who could blame her? But he didn't want this delightful woman to find *him* dull.

He looked at the evidence of her cooking on the countertop, smelled something delicious wafting from the oven.

'And chocolate,' he added. 'The world's best chocolate.'

Now her beautiful brown eyes lit up with interest. *He'd played the right card.*

'Chocolate? You're talking about my favourite food group. So you're from Switzerland?'

He shook his head.

'Belgium? France?' she tried.

'Close,' he said. 'My country is Montovia. A small principality that is not far from those countries.'

She paused, her head tilted to one side. 'You're talking about Montovian chocolate?'

'You know it?' he asked, surprised. His country was known more for its financial services and as a tax haven than for its chocolate and cheese— undoubtedly excellent as they were.

She smiled, revealing delightful dimples in each cheek. He caught his breath. *This Party Queen really was a beauty.*

'Of course I do,' she said. 'Montovian chocolate is sublime. Not easy to get here, but I discovered it when I visited Europe. Nibbled on it, that is. I was a backpacker, and it's too expensive to have much more than a nibble. It's... Well, it's the gold standard of chocolate.'

'I would say the platinum standard,' he said, pleased at her reaction.

'Gold. Platinum. It's just marvellous stuff,' she said. 'Are you a *chocolatier*?'

'No,' he said. 'I am more on the…executive side of the business.' That wasn't stretching the truth too far.

'Is that why you're here in Sydney? The reason for your party? Promoting Montovian chocolate?'

'Among other things,' he said. He didn't want to dig himself in too deep with deception.

She nodded. 'Confidential stuff you can't really talk about?'

'That's right,' he said. He didn't actually like to lie. Evade—*yes*. Lie—*no*.

'Don't worry—you'd be surprised at what secrets we have to keep in the party business,' she said. 'We have to be discreet.'

She put her index finger to her lips. He noticed she didn't wear any rings on either hand.

'But the main reason I am in Sydney is for a vacation,' he said, with 100 per cent truthfulness.

'Really? Who would want a vacation from Montovian chocolate? I don't think I'd ever leave home if I lived in Montovia,' she said with another big smile. 'I'm joking, of course,' she hastened to add.

'No matter how much you love your job, a break is always good.'

'Sydney is a marvellous place for a vacation. I am enjoying it here very much,' he said.

And enjoying it even more since he'd met her. Sydney was a city full of beautiful women, but there was something about Gemma Harper that had instantly appealed to him. Her open, friendly manner, the laughter in her eyes, those dimples, the way she'd tried so unsuccessfully to look ferocious as she'd waved that wooden spoon. She was too pretty to ever look scary. Yet according to his friend Jake, all three of the partners were formidably smart businesswomen. Gemma interested him.

'March is the best time here,' she said. 'It's the start of autumn down-under. Still hot, but not too hot. The sea is warm and perfect for swimming. The school holidays are over. The restaurants are not crowded. I hope you're enjoying our lovely city.' She laughed. 'I sound like I'm spouting a travel brochure, don't I? But, seriously, you're lucky to be here at this time of year.'

The harbourside city was everything Tristan had hoped it would be. But he realised now there was one thing missing from his full enjoyment of Sydney—female company. The life he'd chosen—correction, the life he had had chosen *for* him—meant he often felt lonely.

'You are the lucky one—to live in such a beautiful city on such a magnificent harbour,' he said.

'True. Sydney *is* great, and I love living here,' she said. 'But I'm sure Montovia must be, too. When I think of your chocolate, I picture snow-capped mountains and lakes. Am I right?'

'Yes,' he said. He wanted to tell her more about his home but feared he might trip himself up with an untruth. His experience of life in Montovia was very different from what a tourist might find.

'That was a lucky guess, then,' she said. 'I must confess I don't know anything about your country except for the chocolate.'

'Not many people outside of Europe do, I've discovered,' he said with a shrug.

And that suited him fine in terms of a laid-back vacation. Here in Sydney, half a world away from home, he hadn't been recognised. He liked it that way.

'But perhaps our chocolate will put us on the map down-under.'

'Perhaps after your trip here it will. I think…'

She paused midsentence, frowned. He could almost see the cogs turning.

'The menu for your reception… We'll need to change the desserts to showcase Montovian chocolate. There's still time. I'll get on to it straight away.' She slapped her hand to her mouth. 'Sorry. I jumped the gun there. I meant if you approve, of course.'

'Of course I approve. It's a very good idea. I should have thought of it myself.' Only devising menus was quite out of the range of his experience.

'Excellent. Let me come up with some fabulous chocolate desserts, and I'll pass them by you for approval.'

He was about to tell her not to bother with the approval process when he stopped himself. *He wanted to see her again.* 'Please do that,' he said.

'Eliza shouldn't be too much longer—the traffic can't be that bad. Can I take you into our waiting area? It's not big, but it's more comfortable than standing around here,' she said.

'I am comfortable here,' he said, not liking the idea of her being in a different room from him. 'I like your kitchen.' All stainless steel and large industrial appliances, it still somehow seemed imbued with her warmth and welcome.

Her eyes widened. They were an unusual shade of brown—the colour of cinnamon—and lit up when she smiled.

'Me, too,' she said. 'I have a cake in the oven, and I want to keep an eye on it.'

He inhaled the citrus-scented air. 'It smells very good.'

She glanced at her watch. 'It's a new recipe I'm trying, but I think it will be delicious. I don't know how long you're planning to meet with Eliza for, but the cake won't be ready for another hour or so. Then it has to cool, and then I—'

'I think our meeting will be brief. I have some more sightseeing to do—I've booked a jet boat on the harbour. Perhaps another time I could sample your cake?' He would make certain there would be another time.

'I can see that a cake wouldn't have the same appeal as a jet boat,' she said, with a smile that showed him she did not take offence. 'What else have you seen of Sydney so far?' she asked.

'The usual tourist spots,' he said. 'I've been to the Opera House, Bondi Beach, climbed the Sydney Harbour Bridge.'

'They're all essential. Though I've never found the courage to do the bridge climb. But there's also a Sydney tourists don't get to see. I recommend—'

'Would you show me the Sydney the tourists don't see? I would very much like your company.'

The lovely food director's eyes widened. She hesitated. 'I...I wonder if—'

He was waiting for her reply, when a slender, dark-haired young woman swept into the room. Tristan silently cursed under his breath in his own language at the interruption. She immediately held out her hand to him.

'You must be Mr Marco? I'm so sorry to have kept you waiting—the traffic was a nightmare. I'm Eliza Dunne.'

For a moment he made no acknowledgment of the newcomer's greeting—and then he remembered. He was using Marco as a surname when it was in fact his second given name. He didn't actually have a surname, as such. Not when he was always known simply as Tristan, Crown Prince of Montovia.

CHAPTER TWO

GEMMA CLOSED HER eyes in sheer relief at Eliza's well-timed entrance. *What a lucky escape.* Despite all her resolve not to act on impulse when it came to men, she'd been just about to agree to show Tristan around Sydney.

And that would have been a big mistake.

First, Party Queens had a rule of staff not dating clients. The fact that Andie had broken the rule in spectacular fashion by falling in love with and marrying their billionaire client Dominic Hunt was beside the point. She, Gemma, did not intend to make any exceptions. The business was too important to her for her to make messy mistakes.

But it wasn't just about the company rules. If she'd said yes to Tristan she could have told herself she was simply being hospitable to a foreign visitor—but she would have been lying. And lying to herself about men was a bad habit she was trying to break. She found Tristan way too appealing to pretend that being hospitable was all it would be.

'Thank you for taking care of Mr Marco for me, Gemma,' Eliza said. 'The traffic was crazy—insane.'

'Gemma has looked after me very well,' Tristan said, again with that faint hint of a bow in her direction.

Her heart stepped up a beat at the awareness that shimmered through her.

'She hasn't plied you with cake or muffins or cookies?' asked Eliza with a teasing smile.

'The cake isn't baked yet,' Gemma said. 'But I have cookies and—'

'Perhaps another cake, another time,' Tristan said with a shrug of those broad shoulders, that charming smile. 'And I could give you chocolate in return.'

The shrug. The accent. Those blue, blue eyes. *The Montovian chocolate.*

Yes! her body urged her to shout.

No! urged her common sense.

'Perhaps...' she echoed, the word dwindling away irresolutely.

Thankfully, Eliza diverted Tristan's attention

from her as she engaged him in a discussion about final guest numbers for his party.

Gemma was grateful for some breathing space. Some deep breathing to let her get to grips with the pulse-raising presence of this gorgeous man.

'I'll let you guys chat while I check on my cake,' she said as she went back around the countertop.

She slipped into the pink oven mitts and carefully opened the oven door. As she turned the pan around, she inhaled the sweet-sharp aroma of the cake. Over the years she had learned to gauge the progress of her baking by smell. Its scent told her this cake had a way to go. This kind of solid mud cake needed slow, even cooking.

That was what she'd be looking for in a man in future. A slow burn. Not instant flames. No exhilarating infatuation. No hopping into bed too soon. Rather a long, slow getting to know each other before any kind of commitment—physical or otherwise—was made. The old-fashioned word *courtship* sprang to mind.

She'd managed six months on her own. She was in no rush for the next man. There was no urgency. Next time she wanted to get it right.

Still, no matter what she told herself, Gemma was superaware of Tristan's presence in her kitchen. And, even though he seemed engrossed in his conversation with Eliza, the tension in the way he held himself let her know that he was aware of her, too. The knowledge was a secret pleasure she hugged to herself. It was reassuring that she could still attract a hot guy. Even if there was no way she should do anything about it.

She scraped clean her mixing bowl and spoon and put them in the dishwasher while keeping an ear on Tristan and Eliza's conversation about the party on Friday and an eye on Tristan himself. On those broad shoulders tapering to narrow hips, on the long legs she imagined would be lean and hard with muscle.

Catching her eye, he smiled. Her first instinct was to blush, then smile back. For a long moment their gazes held before she reluctantly dragged hers away and went back to the tricky task of finely slicing strips of candied lemon peel.

Okay, she wasn't in dating exile any more. There was no law to say she couldn't flirt just a little. But she had spent six months fine-tuning her antennae to detect potential heartbreak. And there was something about this handsome Montovian that had those antennae waving wildly with a message of caution. They detected a mystery behind his formal way of speaking and courteous good manners. It wasn't what he'd said but what he *hadn't* said.

Then there was the fact Tristan was only here for a few days. To be a good-looking tourist's vacation fling was *not* what she needed in order to launch herself back into the dating pool. She had to be totally on guard, so she wouldn't fall for the first gorgeous guy who strolled into her life.

She'd learned such painful lessons from her relationship with Alistair. It had been love at first sight for both of them—or so she'd thought. Followed by an emotional rollercoaster that had lasted for eighteen months. Too blinded by desire, love—whatever that turbulent mix of emotions had been—she'd only seen the Alistair she'd wanted to see. She had missed all the cues that would have alerted her he wasn't what he'd sworn he was.

She'd heard the rumours before she'd started to date him. But he'd assured her that he'd kicked his cocaine habit—*and* his reputation as a player. When time after time he'd lapsed, she'd always forgiven him, given him the one more chance he'd begged for. And then another. After all, she'd loved him and he'd loved her—hadn't he?

Then had come the final hurt and humiliation of finding him in the bathroom at a party with a so-called 'mutual friend'. Doing *her* as well as the drugs. Gemma doubted she'd ever be able to scour that image from her eyes.

After that there'd been no more chances, no more Alistair. She'd spent the last six months trying to sort out why she always seemed to fall for the wrong type of man. Her dating history was littered with misfires—though none as heart-wrenchingly painful as Alistair's betrayal.

On her first day back in the dating world she wasn't going to backtrack. Tristan was still a mystery man. He had perhaps not been completely honest about himself and was on vacation from a faraway country. How many more strikes against him could there be?

But, oh, he was handsome.

Eliza had suggested that Tristan follow her into her office. But he turned towards Gemma. 'I would like to speak to Gemma again first, please,' he said, with unmistakable authority.

Eliza sent Gemma a narrow-eyed, speculative glance. 'Sure,' she said to Tristan. 'My office is just around the corner. I'll wait for you there.'

Gemma could hear the sound of her own heart

beating in the sudden silence of the room as Eliza left. Her mouth went dry as Tristan came closer to face her over the countertop.

His gaze was very direct. 'So, Gemma, you did not get a chance to answer me—will you show me your home town?'

It took every bit of resolve for her not to run around to the other side of the countertop and babble, *Of course. How about we start right now?*

Instead she wiped her suddenly clammy hands down the sides of her apron. Took a deep breath to steady her voice. 'I'm sorry, Tristan. But I...I can't.'

He looked taken aback. She got the distinct impression he wasn't used to anyone saying *no* to him.

He frowned. 'You are sure?'

'It wouldn't be...appropriate,' she said.

'Because I am a client?' he asked, his gaze direct on hers.

She shifted from foot to foot, clad in the chef's clogs she wore in the kitchen. 'That's right,' she said. 'I'm sorry, but it's company policy.'

Just for a moment, did disappointment cloud those blue eyes? 'That is a shame. As I said, I would very much enjoy your company.'

'I…well, I would enjoy yours, too. But…uh… rules are rules.'

Such rules *could* be broken—as Andie had proved. But Gemma was determined to stick to her resolve, even if it was already tinged with regret.

His mouth twisted. 'I know all about rules that have to be followed whether one likes it or not,' he said with an edge to his voice. 'I don't like it, but I understand.'

What did he mean by that? Gemma wasn't sure if he was referring to the Party Queens rules or a different set of rules that might apply to him. She sensed there might be a lot she didn't understand about him. And now would never get a chance to.

'Thank you,' she said. 'I'll email the amended dessert menu to you.'

'Dessert menu?'

'Using Montovian chocolate for your party,' she prompted.

'Of course,' he said. 'I will look forward to it. I am sorry I will not be seeing more of Sydney with you.'

'I…I'm sorry, too.' But she would not toss away all that hard work she'd done on her insecurities.

'Now I must let you get back to work while I

speak with Eliza,' he said, in what sounded very much like dismissal.

Gemma refused to admire his back view as he left the kitchen. *She liked a nice butt on a man.* For better or for worse, that ship had sailed. And she felt good about her decision. She really did.

But she was on edge as she prepared the coconut frosting by melting white chocolate and beating it with coconut cream. She kept glancing up, in case Tristan came back into the room. Was so distracted she grated the edge of her finger as well as the fine slivers of lemon and lime peel that would give the frosting its bite. But a half-hour later, when his meeting with Eliza concluded, he only briefly acknowledged her as he passed by the doorway to her kitchen.

She gripped her hands so tightly her fingernails cut into her hands. The sudden feeling of loss was totally irrational. She would *not* run after him to say she'd changed her mind.

An hour later, as Gemma was finishing her work on the cake, Eliza popped her head around the door.

'Cake ready?' she asked. 'The smell of it has been driving me crazy.'

'Nearly ready. I've been playing with the candied peel on top and tidying up the frosting,' Gemma said. 'Come and have a look. I think it will be perfect for the Sanderson wedding.'

'Magnificent,' Eliza said. She sneaked a quick taste of the leftover frosting from the bowl. 'Mmm…coconut. Nice touch. You really are a genius when it comes to food.'

Gemma knew her mouth had turned downwards. 'Just not such a genius when it comes to guys.'

Eliza patted her on the shoulder. 'Come on—you've done so well with your sabbatical. Aren't we going to celebrate your freedom to date—I mean to date *wisely*—with this cake?'

Both Gemma and Andie had been totally supportive during her man break. Had proved themselves again and again to be good friends as well as business partners.

Gemma nodded. 'I know…' she said, unable to stop the catch in her voice. It was the right thing to have turned down Tristan's invitation, but that didn't stop a lingering sense of regret, of wondering *what might have been.*

'What's brought on this fit of the gloomies?' Eliza asked. 'Oh, wait—don't tell me. The handsome mystery man—Tristan Marco. He's just your type, isn't he? As soon as I saw him, I thought—'

Gemma put up her hand to stop her. 'In looks, yes, I can't deny that. He's really hot.' She forced a smile. 'Our guesses about him were *so* far off the mark, weren't they?'

'He's about as far away from short, bald and middle-aged as he could be,' Eliza agreed. 'I had to stop myself staring at him for fear he'd think I was incredibly bad mannered.'

'You can imagine how shocked I was when he told me *he* was our client for the Friday night party. But I don't think he told me everything. There's still a lot of the mystery man about him.'

'What do you mean, *still* too much mystery? What did you talk about here in your kitchen?'

Gemma filled Eliza in on her conversation with Tristan, leaving out his invitation for her to show him around Sydney. Eliza would only remind her that dating clients was a no-no. And, besides, she didn't want to talk about it—she'd made her decision.

Eliza nodded. 'He told me much the same thing—although he was quite evasive about the final list of guests. But what the heck? It's his party, and he can invite anyone he wants to it as long as he sticks with the number we quoted on. We're ahead financially, so it's all good to me.'

'That reminds me,' Gemma said. 'I have to amend the desserts for Friday to include Montovian chocolate. And he needs to approve them.'

'You can discuss the menu change with him on Wednesday.'

Gemma stopped, the blunt palette knife she'd used to apply the frosting still in her hand. 'Wednesday? Why Wednesday?'

'Tristan is on vacation in Sydney. He's asked me to book a private yacht cruise around the harbour on Wednesday. And to organise an elegant, romantic lunch for two to be taken on board.'

A romantic lunch for two?

Gemma let go of the palette knife so it landed with a clatter on the stainless steel benchtop, using the distraction to gather her thoughts. So she'd been right to distrust mystery man Tristan. He'd asked her to show him around Sydney. And at the same time he was making plans for a romantic tryst with another woman on a luxury yacht.

Thank heaven she'd said *no*.

Or had she misread him? Had his interest only been in her knowledge of local hotspots? After a six-month sabbatical, maybe her dating skills were so rusty she'd mistaken his meaning.

Still, she couldn't help feeling annoyed. Not so much at Tristan but at herself, for having let down her guard even if only momentarily. If she'd glimpsed that look of interest in *his* eyes, he would have seen it in *hers*.

'Which boat did you book?' she asked Eliza.

The cooking facilities on the charter yachts available in Sydney Harbour ranged from a basic galley to a full-sized luxury kitchen.

'Because it will be midweek, I managed to get the *Argus* on short notice.'

'Wow! Well done. He should love that.'

'He did. I showed him a choice of boats online, but the *Argus* was the winner hands down.'

'His date should be really impressed,' Gemma said, fighting off an urge to sound snarky.

'I think that was the idea—the lucky lady.'

The *Argus* was a replica of a sixty-foot vintage wooden motor yacht from the nineteen-twenties and the ultimate in luxury. Its hourly hire rate was a mind-boggling amount of dollars. To book it for just two people was a total extravagance. Party Queens had organised a corporate client's event for thirty people on the boat at the start of summer. It was classy, high-tech and had a fully equipped kitchen. Tristan must *really* want to impress his date.

'So I'm guessing if lunch is on the *Argus* we won't be on a tight budget.'

'He told me to "spend what it takes",' said Eliza with a delighted smile. The more dollars for Party Queens, the happier Eliza was.

Gemma gritted her teeth and forced herself to think of Tristan purely as a client, not as an attractive man who'd caught her eye. It would be better if she still thought of him as bald with a pot belly. 'It's short notice, but of course we can do it. Any restrictions on the menu?'

Planning party menus could involve dealing with an overwhelming array of food allergies and intolerances.

'None that he mentioned,' said Eliza.

'That makes things easier.' Gemma thought out loud. 'An elegant on-board lunch for two…I'm thinking seafood—fresh and light. A meal we can prep ahead and our chef can finish off on board. We'll book the waiter today.'

'"Romantic" is the keyword, remember? And he wants the best French champagne—which, of course, I'll organise.' Eliza had an interest in wine as well as in spreadsheets.

'I wonder who his guest is?' Gemma said, hoping she wouldn't betray her personal interest to Eliza.

'Again, he didn't say,' Eliza said.

Gemma couldn't help a stab of envy towards Tristan's date, for whom he was making such an effort to be *romantic.* But he was a client. And she was a professional. If he wanted romantic, she'd give him romantic. In spades.

'But tell me—why will *I* be meeting with Tristan on Wednesday?'

'He wants you to be on board for the duration— to make sure everything is perfect. His words, not mine.'

'What? A lunch for two with a chef and a waiter doesn't need a supervisor, as well. You know how carefully we vet the people who work for us. They can be trusted to deliver the Party Queens' promise.'

Eliza put up her hands in a placatory gesture. 'Relax. I know that. I know the yacht comes with skipper and crew. But Tristan asked for you to be on board, too. He wants you to make sure everything goes well.'

'No!' Gemma said and realised her protest sounded over-the-top. 'I...I mean there's no need for me to be there at all. I'll go over everything with the chef and the waiter to make sure the presentation and service is faultless.'

Eliza shook her head. 'Not good enough. Tristan Marco has specifically requested your presence on board.'

Gemma knew the bottom line was always important to Eliza. She'd made sure their business was a success financially. With a sinking heart Gemma realised there would be no getting out of this. And Eliza was only too quick to confirm that.

'You know how lucrative his party on Friday is for us, Gemma. Tristan is an important client. You really have to do this. Whether you like it or not.'

CHAPTER THREE

ON WEDNESDAY MORNING Gemma made her way along the harbourside walk on the northern shore of Sydney Harbour. Milson's Point and the Art Deco North Sydney Swimming Pool were behind her as she headed towards the wharf at Lavender Bay, where she was to join the *Argus*. As she walked she realised why she felt so out of sorts— she was jealous of Tristan's unknown date. And put out that he had replaced her so quickly.

It wasn't that she was jealous of the other woman's cruise on a magnificent yacht on beautiful Sydney Harbour. Or the superb meal she would be served, thanks to the skill of the Party Queens team. No. What Gemma envied her most for was the pleasure of Tristan's company.

Gemma seethed with a most unprofessional indignation at the thought of having to dance attendance on the couple's romantic rendezvous. There was no justification for her feelings—Tristan had asked to spend time with her and she had turned him down. In fact, her feelings were more than a touch irrational. But still she didn't like the idea of seeing Tristan with another woman.

She did not want to do this.

Why had he insisted on her presence on board? This was a romantic lunch for *two*, for heaven's sake. There was only so much for her to do for a simple three-course meal. She would have too much time to observe Tristan being charming to his date. *And, oh, how charming the man could be.*

If she was forced to watch him kiss that other woman, she might just have to jump off board and brave the sharks and jellyfish to swim to shore.

Suck it up, Gemma, you turned him down.

She forced herself to remember that she was the director of her own company, looking after an important client. To convince herself that there were worse things to do than twiddle her thumbs in the lap of luxury on one of the most beautiful harbours in the world on a perfect sunny day. And to remind herself to paste a convincing smile on her face as she did everything in her power to make her client's day a success.

As she rounded the boardwalk past Luna Park fun fair, she picked up her pace when she no-

ticed the *Argus* had already docked at Lavender
Bay. The charter company called it a 'gentleman's
cruiser', and the wooden boat's vintage lines made
it stand out on a harbour dotted with slick, modern watercraft. She didn't know much about boats,
but she liked this one—it looked fabulous, and
it had a very well-fitted-out kitchen that was a
dream to work in.

The Lavender Bay wharf was on the western
side of the Sydney Harbour Bridge, virtually in its
shadow, with a view right through to the gleaming white sails of the Opera House on the eastern
side. The water was unbelievably blue to match
the blue sky. The air was tangy with salt. How
could she stay down on a day like this? *She would
make the most of it.*

Gemma got her smile ready as she reached the
historic old dock. She expected that a crew member would greet her and help her on board. But her
heart missed a beat when she saw it was Tristan
who stood there. Tristan…in white linen trousers and a white shirt open at the neck to reveal
a glimpse of muscular chest, sleeves rolled back
to show strong, sinewy forearms. Tristan looking
tanned and unbelievably handsome, those blue

eyes putting the sky to shame. Her heart seemed almost literally to leap into her throat.

She had never been more attracted to a man.

'Let me help you,' he said in his deep, accented voice as he extended a hand to help her across the gangplank.

She looked at his hand for a long moment, not sure what her reaction would be at actually touching him. But she knew she would need help to get across because she felt suddenly shaky and weak at the knees. She swallowed hard against a painful swell of regret.

What an idiot she'd been to say no *to him.*

Gemma looked as lovely as he remembered, Tristan thought as he held out his hand to her. Even lovelier—which he hadn't thought possible. Her auburn hair fell to her shoulders, glinting copper and gold in the sunlight. Her narrow deep blue cut-off pants and blue-and-white-striped top accentuated her curves in a subtle way he appreciated. But her smile was tentative, and she had hesitated before taking his hand and accepting his help to come on board.

'Gemma, it is so good to see you,' he said while his heart beat a tattoo of exultation that she had come—and he sent out a prayer that she would forgive him for insisting in such an autocratic manner on her presence.

She had her rules—he had his. His rules decreed that spending time with a girl like Gemma could lead nowhere. But he hadn't been able to stop thinking about her. So her rules had had to be bent.

'The Party Queens motto is No Job Too Big or Too Small,' Gemma said as she stepped on board. 'This...this is a very small job.'

He realised he was holding her hand for longer than would be considered polite. That her eyes were flickering away from the intensity of his gaze. But he didn't want to let go of her hand.

'Small...but important.' Incredibly important to him as the clock ticked relentlessly away on his last days of freedom.

She abruptly released her hand from his. Her lush mouth tightened. 'Is it? Then I hope you'll be happy with the menu.'

'Your chef and waiter are already in the kitchen,' he said. 'You have created a superb lunch for us.'

'And your guest for lunch? Is she—?'

At that moment a crew member approached to

tell him they were ready to cast off from the dock and start their cruise around the harbour.

Tristan thanked him and turned to Gemma. 'I'm very much looking forward to this,' he said. *To getting to know her.*

'You couldn't have a better day for exploring the harbour,' she said with a wave of her hand that encompassed the impossibly blue waters, the boats trailing frothy white wakes behind them, the blue sky unmarred by clouds.

'The weather is perfect,' he said. 'Did Party Queens organise that for me, too?'

It was a feeble attempt at humour and he knew it. Gemma seemed to know it, too.

But her delightful dimples flirted in her cheeks as she replied, 'We may have cast a good weather spell or two.'

He raised his eyebrows. 'So you have supernatural powers? The Party Queens continue to surprise me.'

'I'd be careful who you're calling a witch,' she said with a deepening of the dimples. 'Andie and Eliza might not like it.'

A witch? She had bewitched him, all right. He had never felt such an instant attraction to a woman. Especially one so deeply unsuitable.

'And you?' In his country's mythology the most powerful witches had red hair and green eyes. This bewitching Australian had eyes the colour of cinnamon—warm and enticing. 'Are *you* a witch, Gemma Harper?' he asked slowly.

She met his gaze directly as they stood facing each other on the deck, the dock now behind them. 'I like to think I'm a witch in the kitchen— or it could be that I just have a highly developed intuition for food. But if you want to think I conjured up these blue skies, go right ahead. All part of the service.'

'So there is no limit to your talents?' he said.

'You're darn right about that,' she said with an upward tilt of her chin.

For a long moment their eyes met. Her heart-shaped face, so new to him, seemed already familiar—possibly because she had not been out of his thoughts since the moment they'd met. He ached to lift his hand and trace the freckles scattered across the bridge of her nose with his finger, then explore the contours of her mouth, her top lip with its perfect, plump bow. *He ached to kiss her.*

But there could be no kissing. Not with this girl, who had captured his interest within seconds of meeting her. Not when there were rules and strictures guiding the way he spent his life. When there were new levels of responsibility he had to step up to when he returned home. He was on a deadline—everything would change when he turned thirty, in three months' time. These next few days in Sydney were the last during which he could call his time his own.

His life had been very different before the accident that had killed his brother. Before the *spare* had suddenly become the *heir*. His carefree and some might even say hedonistic life as the second son had been abruptly curtailed.

There had been unsuitable girlfriends—forbidden to him now. He had taken risks on the racing-car circuit and on horseback, had scaled the mountains that towered over Montovia. Now everything he did came under scrutiny. The Crown took priority over everything. Duty had always governed part of his life. Now it was to be his all.

But he had demanded to be allowed to take this vacation—insisted on this last freedom before he had to buckle under to duty. To responsibility. For the love of his country.

His fascination with Gemma Harper was nowhere on the approved official agenda...

'I'm trying to imagine what other feats of magic you can perform,' he said, attempting to come to terms with the potent spell she had cast on him. The allure of her lush mouth. The warmth of her eyes. The inexplicable longing for her that had led him to planning this day.

He should not be thinking this way about a commoner.

She bit her lip, took a step back from him. 'My magic trick is to make sure your lunch date goes smoothly. But I don't need a fairy's wand for that.' Her dimples disappeared. 'I want everything to be to your satisfaction. Are you happy with the *Argus*?'

Her voice was suddenly stilted, as if she had extracted the laughter and levity from it. *Back to business* was the message. And she was right. A business arrangement. That was all there should be between them.

'It's a very handsome boat,' he said. He was used to millionaire's toys. Took this level of luxury for granted. But that didn't stop him appreciating it. And he couldn't put a price on the spectacular view. 'I'm very happy with it for this purpose.'

'Good. The *Argus* is my favourite of any of the boats we've worked on,' she said. 'I love its wonderful Art Deco style. It's from another era of graciousness.'

'Would you like me to show you around?' he said.

If she said yes, he would make only a cursory inspection of the luxury bedrooms, the grand stateroom. He did not want her to get the wrong idea. Or to torture himself with thoughts of what could never be.

She shook her head. 'No need. I'm familiar with the layout,' she said. 'We held a corporate party here earlier in the spring. I'd like to catch up with my staff now.'

'Your waiter has already set up for lunch on the deck.'

'I'd like to see how it looks,' she said.

She had a large tan leather bag slung over her shoulder. 'Let me take your bag for you,' he said.

'Thank you, but I'm fine,' she said, clutching on to the strap.

'I insist,' he said. The habits of courtliness and chivalry towards women had been bred into him.

She shrugged. 'Okay.' Reluctantly, she handed it to him.

The weight of her bag surprised him, and he

pretended to stagger on the deck. 'What have you got in here? An arsenal of wooden spoons?'

Her eyes widened, and she laughed. 'Of course not.'

'So I don't need to seek out my armour?'

It was tempting to tell her about the suits of medieval armour in the castle he called home. As a boy he'd thought everyone had genuine armour to play with—it hadn't been until he was older that he'd become aware of his uniquely privileged existence. Privileged and restricted.

But he couldn't reveal his identity to her yet. He wanted another day of just being plain Tristan. Just a guy getting to know a girl.

'Of course you don't need armour. Besides, I wasn't actually going to *hit* you with that wooden spoon, you know.'

'You had me worried back in that kitchen,' he teased. He was getting used to speaking English again, relaxing into the flow of words.

'I don't believe that for a second,' she said. 'You're so much bigger than me, and—'

'And what?'

'I...I trusted that you wouldn't hurt me.'

He had to clear his throat. 'I would never hurt you,' he said. And yet he wasn't being honest with her. Inadvertently, he *could* hurt her. But it would not be by intent. *This was just one day.*

'So what's really in the bag?' he asked.

'It's only bits and pieces of my favourite kitchen equipment—just in case I might need them.'

'Just in case the chef can't do his job?' he asked.

'You *did* want me here to supervise,' she said, her laughter gone as he reminded her of why she thought she was on board. 'And supervise I need to. Please. I have to see where we will be serving lunch.'

There was a formal dining area inside the cabin, but Tristan was glad Party Queens had chosen to serve lunch at an informal area with the best view at the fore of the boat. Under shelter from the sun and protected from the breeze. The very professional waiter had already set an elegant table with linen mats, large white plates and gleaming silver.

Gemma nodded in approval when she saw it. Then straightened a piece of cutlery into perfect alignment with another without seeming to be aware she was doing it.

'Our staff have done their usual good job,' she said. 'We'll drop anchor at Store Beach at lunchtime. That will be very *romantic*.'

She stressed the final word with a tight twist of her lips that surprised him.

'I don't know where Store Beach is, but I'm looking forward to seeing it,' he said.

'It's near Manly, which is a beachside suburb— the start of our wonderful northern beaches. Store Beach is a secluded beach accessible only from the water. I'm sure you and your…uh…*date* will like it.' She glanced at her watch. 'In the meantime, it's only ten o'clock. We can set up for morning tea or coffee now, if you'd like?'

'Coffee would be good,' he said. Sydney had surprised him in many ways—not least of which was with its excellent European-style coffee.

Gemma gave the table setting another tweak and then stepped away from it. 'All that's now lacking is your guest. Are we picking her up from another wharf, or is she already on board?'

'She's already on board,' he said.

'Oh…' she said. 'Is she—?' She turned to look towards the passageway that led to the living area and bedrooms.

'She's not down there,' he said.

'Then where—?'

He sought the correct words. 'She…she's right here,' he said.

'I don't see anyone.' She frowned. 'I don't get it.'

He cleared his throat. '*You* are my guest for lunch, Gemma.'

She stilled. For a long moment she didn't say anything. Tristan shifted from foot to foot. He couldn't tell if she was pleased or annoyed.

'*Me?*' she said finally, in a voice laced with disbelief.

'You said there was a rule about you not spending time outside of work with clients. So I arranged to have time with you while you were officially at work.'

Her shoulders were held hunched and high. 'You…you tricked me. I don't like being tricked.'

'You could call it that—and I apologise for the deception. But there didn't seem to be another way. I had to see you again, Gemma.'

She took a deep intake of breath. 'Why didn't you just ask me?'

'Would you have said "yes"?'

She bowed her head. 'Perhaps not.'

'I will ask you now. Will you be my guest for lunch on board the *Argus*?'

She looked down at the deck.

He reached out his hand and tilted her chin upwards so she faced him. 'Please?'

He could see the emotions dancing across her face. Astonishment. A hint of anger. And could that be relief?

Her shoulders relaxed, and her dimples made a brief appearance in the smoothness of her cheeks. 'I guess as you have me trapped on board I have no choice but to say "yes".'

'Trapped? I don't wish you to feel trapped...' He didn't want to seem arrogant and domineering—job descriptions that came with the role of crown prince. His brother had fulfilled them impeccably. They sat uncomfortably with Tristan. 'Gemma, if this is unacceptable to you, I'll ask the captain to turn back to Lavender Bay. You can get off. Is that what you want?'

She shook her head. 'No. That's not what I want. I...I want to be here with you. In fact, I can't tell you how happy I am there's no other woman. I might have been tempted to throw her overboard.'

Her peal of laughter that followed was delightful, and it made him smile in response.

'Surely you wouldn't do that?'

She looked up at him, her eyes dancing with new confidence. 'You might be surprised at what I'm capable of,' she murmured. 'You don't know me at all, Tristan.'

'I hope to remedy that today,' he said.

Already he knew that this single day he'd permitted himself to share with her would not be enough. He had to anchor his feet to the deck so he didn't swing her into his arms. He must truly be bewitched. Because he couldn't remember when he'd last felt such anticipation at the thought of spending time with a woman.

'Welcome aboard, Gemma,' he said—and had to stop himself from sweeping into a courtly bow.

CHAPTER FOUR

GEMMA COULDN'T STOP SMILING—in relief, anticipation and a slowly bubbling excitement. After all
that angst, *she* was Tristan's chosen date for the
romantic lunch. *She* was the one he'd gone to so
much effort and expense to impress. The thought
made her heart skitter with wonder and more than
a touch of awe.

She'd joked about casting spells, but *something*
had happened back there in her kitchen—some
kind of connection between her and Tristan that
was quite out of the ordinary. It seemed he had
felt it, too. She ignored the warning of the insistent twitching of her antennae. This magical
feeling was *not* just warm and fuzzy lust born
from Tristan's incredible physical appeal and the
fact that she was coming out of a six-month man
drought.

Oh, on a sensual level she wanted him, all
right—her knees were still shaky just from the

touch of his hand gripping hers as he'd helped her across the gangplank. But she didn't want Tristan just as a gorgeous male body to satisfy physical hunger. *It was something so much deeper than that.* Which was all kinds of crazy when he was only going to be around for a short time. And was still as much of a mystery to her as he had been the day they'd met.

For her, this was something more than just physical attraction. But what about him? Was this just a prelude to seduction? Was he a handsome guy with all the right words—spoken in the most charming of accents—looking for a no-strings holiday fling?

She tried to think of all those 'right' reasons for staying away from Tristan but couldn't remember one of them. By tricking her into this lunch with him, he had taken the decision out of her hands. But there was no need to get carried away. This was no big deal. *It was only lunch.* It would be up to her to say *no* if this was a net cast to snare her into a one-night stand.

She reached up and kissed him lightly on the cheek in an effort to make it casual. 'Thank you.'

She was rewarded by the relief in his smile. 'It is absolutely my pleasure,' he said.

'Does Eliza know?' she asked. *Had her friend been in on this deception?*

Tristan shook his head. 'I didn't tell her why I wanted you on board. I sense she's quite protective of you. I didn't want anything to prevent you from coming today.'

Of course Eliza was protective of her. Andie, too. Her friends had been there to pick up the pieces after the Alistair fallout. Eliza had seemed impressed with Tristan, though—impressed with him as a client...maybe not so impressed with him as a candidate for Gemma's first foray back into the dating world. He was still in many ways their Mr Mystery. *But she could find out more about him today.*

'I did protest that I wasn't really needed,' she said, still secretly delighted at the way things had turned out. 'Not when there are a chef and a waiter and a crew on the boat.'

'I'm sure the bonus I added to the Party Queens fee guaranteed your presence on board. She's a shrewd businesswoman, your partner.'

'Yes, she is,' Gemma agreed. No wonder Eliza hadn't objected to Gemma's time being so wastefully spent. How glad she was now that Eliza had insisted she go. But she felt as though the tables had been turned on her, and she wasn't quite sure where she stood.

She looked up at Tristan. Her heart flipped over at how handsome he was, with the sea breeze ruffling his hair, his eyes such a vivid blue against his tan. He looked totally at home on this multi-million-dollar boat, seemingly not impressed by the luxury that surrounded them. She wondered what kind of world he came from. One where money was not in short supply, she guessed.

'I...I'm so pleased about this...this turn of events,' she said. 'Thrilled, in fact. But how do we manage it? I...I feel a bit like Cinderella. One minute I'm in the kitchen, the next minute I'm at the ball.'

He seemed amused by her flight of fancy, and he smiled. What was it about his smile that appealed so much? His perfect teeth? The warmth in his eyes? The way his face creased into lines of good humour?

'I guess you could see it like that...' he said.

'And if I'm Cinderella...I guess *you're* the prince.'

His smile froze, and tension suddenly edged his voice. 'What...what do you mean?'

Gemma felt a sudden chill that was not a sea breeze. It perplexed her. 'Cinderella... The ball... The prince... The pumpkin transformed into a carriage... You know...' she said, gesturing with her hands. 'Don't you have the story of Cinderella in your country?'

'Uh...of course,' he said with an obvious relief that puzzled her. 'Those old fairytales originally came from Europe.'

So she'd unwittingly said the wrong thing? Maybe he thought she had expectations of something more than a day on the harbour. Of getting her claws into him. She really was out of practice. At dating. At flirting. Simply talking with a man who attracted her.

'I meant... Well, I meant that Cinderella meets the prince and you...well, you're as handsome as any fairytale prince and... Never mind.'

She glanced down at her white sneakers, tied with jaunty blue laces. Maybe this wasn't the time to be making a joke about a glass slipper.

Tristan nodded thoughtfully. 'Of course. And I found Cinderella in her kitchen...'

She felt uncomfortable about carrying this any further. He seemed to be making too much effort to join in the story. His English was excellent, but maybe he'd missed the nuances of the analogy. Maybe he had trouble with her Australian accent.

'Yes. And talking of kitchens, I need to talk to the chef and—' She made to turn back towards the door that led inside the cabin.

Tristan reached out and put his hand on her arm to stop her.

'You don't need to do anything but enjoy yourself,' he said, his tone now anything but uncertain. 'I've spoken to your staff. They know that you are my honoured guest.'

He dropped his hand from her arm so she could turn back to face him. 'You said that? You called me your "honoured guest"?' There was something about his formal way of speaking that really appealed to her. His words made her want to preen with pleasure.

'I did—and they seemed pleased,' he said.

Party Queens had a policy of only hiring staff they personally liked. The freelance chef on board today was a guy she'd worked with in her restaurant days. But it was the Australian way to be irreverent... She suspected she might be teased about this sudden switch from staff to guest. Especially having lunch in the company of such an exceptionally good-looking man.

'They were pleased I'm out of their hair?' she asked.

'Pleased for *you*. They obviously hold their boss in high regard.'

'That's nice,' she said, nodding.

Hospitality could be a tense business at times, what with deadlines and temperamental clients and badly behaving guests. It was good to have it affirmed that the staff respected her.

'What about lunch?' she said, indicating the direction of the kitchen. 'The—?'

Tristan waved her objections away. 'Relax, Gemma.' A smile hovered at the corners of his mouth. As if he were only too aware of how difficult she found it to give up control of her job. 'I'm the host. You are my guest. Forget about what's going on in the kitchen. Just enjoy being the guest—not the party planner.'

'This might take some getting used to,' she said with a rueful smile. 'But thank you, yes.'

'Good,' he said.

'I'm not sure of one thing,' she said. 'Do you still want me as your tour guide? If that's the case, I need to be pointing out some sights to you.'

She turned from him, took a few steps to the railing and looked out, the breeze lifting her hair from her face.

'On the right—oh, hang on…don't we say "starboard" on a boat? To *starboard* are the Finger Wharves at Walsh Bay. The configuration is like a hand—you know, with each wharf a finger. The wharves are home to the Sydney Theatre Company. It's a real experience to go to the theatre there and—'

'Stop!'

She turned, to see Tristan with his hand held up in a halt sign. His hands were attractive, large with long elegant fingers. Yes, nice hands were an asset on a man, too. She wondered how they would feel—

She could not go there.

Gemma knew she'd been chattering on too much about the wharves. Gabbling, in fact. But she suddenly felt…*nervous* in Tristan's presence. And chatter had always been her way of distancing herself from an awkward situation.

She spluttered to a halt. 'You don't want to know about the wharves? Okay, on the left-hand side—I mean the *port* side—is Luna Park and…'

Tristan lowered his hand. Moved closer to her.

So close they were just kissing distance apart. She tried not to look at his mouth. That full lower lip... the upper lip slightly narrower. *A sensual mouth was another definite asset in a man.* So was his ability to kiss.

She flushed and put her hand to her forehead. Why was she letting her thoughts run riot on what Tristan would be like to kiss? She took a step back, only to feel the railing press into her back. It was a little scary that she was thinking this way about a man she barely knew.

'There's no need for you to act like a tour guide,' he said. 'The first day I got here I took a guided tour of the harbour.'

'But you asked me to show you the insider's Sydney. The Wharf Theatre is a favourite place of mine and—'

'That was just a ploy,' he said.

Gemma caught her breath. 'A ploy?'

'I had to see you again. I thought there was more chance of you agreeing to show me around than if I straight out asked you to dinner.'

'Oh,' she said, momentarily lost for words.

'Or...or lunch on the harbour?'

Her heart started to thud so hard she thought surely he must hear it—even over the faint thrumming of the boat's motor, the sound of people calling out to each other on the cruiser that was passing them, the squawk of the seagulls wheeling over the harbour wall, where a fisherman had gutted his catch.

'That is correct,' Tristan said.

'So…so you had to find another way?' To think that all the time she'd spent thinking about *him*, he'd been thinking about *her*.

For the first time Gemma detected a crack in Tristan's self-assured confidence. His hands were thrust deep into the pockets of his white trousers. 'I…I had to see if you were as…as wonderful as I remembered,' he said, and his accent was more pronounced.

She loved the way he rolled his r*'s.* Without that accent, without the underlying note of sincerity, his words might have sounded sleazy. But they didn't. They sent a shiver of awareness and anticipation up her spine.

'And…and are you disappointed?'

She wished now that she'd worn something less utilitarian than a T-shirt—even though it was a very smart, fitted T-shirt, with elbow-length sleeves—and sneakers. They were work clothes. Not 'lunching with a hot guy' clothes. Still, if she'd had to dress with the thought of impressing Tristan, she might still be back at her apartment, with the contents of her wardrobe scattered all over the bed.

'Not at all,' he said.

He didn't need to say the words. The appreciation in his eyes said it all. Her hand went to her heart to steady its out-of-control thud.

'Me neither. I mean, I'm not disappointed in *you*.' *Aargh, could she sound any dumber?* 'I thought you were pretty wonderful, too. I...I regretted that I knocked back your request for me to show you around. But...but I had my reasons.'

His dark eyebrows rose. 'Reasons? Not just the company rules?'

'Those, too. When we first started the business, we initiated a "no dating the clients" rule. It made sense.'

'Yet I believe your business partner Andie married a client, so that rule cannot be set in concrete.'

'How did you know that?' She answered her own question, 'Of course—Jake Marlowe.' The best friend of the groom. 'You're right. But Andie was the exception.' Up until now there had been no client who had made *Gemma* want to bend the rules.

'And the other reasons?'

'Personal. I…I came out of a bad relationship more…more than a little wounded.'

'I'm sorry to hear that.' His eyes searched her face. 'And now?'

She took a deep breath. Finally she had that heartbeat under control. 'I've got myself sorted,' she said, not wanting to give any further explanation.

'You don't wear a ring. I assumed you were single.' He paused. '*Are* you single?'

Gemma was a bit taken aback by the directness of his question. 'Very single,' she said. Did that sound too enthusiastic? As if she were making certain he knew she was available?

Gemma curled her hands into fists. She had to stop second guessing everything she said. Tristan had thought she was wonderful in her apron, all flushed from the heat of the oven and without a scrap of make-up. She had to be herself. Not try and please a man by somehow attempting to be what he wanted her to be. She'd learned that from her mother—and it was difficult to unlearn.

Her birth father had died before she was born and her mother, Aileen, had brought Gemma up on her own until she was six. Then her mother had met Dennis.

He had never wanted children but had grudgingly accepted Gemma as part of a package deal when he'd married Aileen. Her mother had trained Gemma to be grateful to her stepfather for having taken her on. To keep him happy by always being a sweet little girl, by forgiving his moody behaviour, his lack of real affection.

Gemma had become not necessarily a *people* pleaser but a man pleaser. She believed that was why she'd put up with Alistair's bad behaviour for so long. It was a habit she was determined to break.

She decided to take charge of the conversation. 'What about you, Tristan? Are you single, too?'

He nodded. 'Yes.'

'Have you ever been married?'

'No,' he said. 'I...I haven't met the right woman. And you?'

'Same. I haven't met the right man.' Boy, had she met some wrong ones. But those days were past. *No more heartbreakers.*

The swell from a passing ferry made her rock unsteadily on her feet as she swayed with the sudden motion of the boat.

Tristan caught her elbow to steady her. 'You okay?' he said.

The action brought him close to her. So close she could feel the strength in his body, smell the fresh scent of him that hinted at sage and woodlands and the mountain country he came from. There was something so *different* about him—almost a sense of *other*. It intrigued her, excited her.

'F-fine, thank you,' she stuttered.

His grip, though momentary, had been firm and warm on her arm, and her reaction to the contact disconcerted her. She found herself trembling a little. Those warning antennae waved so wildly she felt light-headed. She shouldn't be feeling this intense attraction to someone she knew so little about. *It was against her every resolve.*

She took another steadying breath, as deep as she could without looking too obvious. The *Argus* had left the Harbour Bridge behind. 'We're on home territory for me now,' she said, in a determinedly conversational tone. 'Come over to this side and I'll show you.'

'You live around here?' he said as he followed her.

'See over there?' She waved to encompass the park that stretched to the water under the massive supports for the bridge overhead, the double row of small shops, the terraced houses, the multi-million-dollar apartments that sat at the edge of the water. 'You can just see the red-tiled roof of my humble apartment block.'

Tristan walked over to the railing, leaned his elbows on the top, looked straight ahead. Gemma stood beside him, very aware that their shoulders were almost nudging.

'Sydney does not disappoint me,' he said finally.

'I'm glad to hear that,' she said. 'What made you come here on your vacation?'

He shrugged. 'Australia is a place I always wanted to see. So far from Europe. Like the last frontier.'

Again, Gemma sensed he was leaving out more than he was saying. Her self-protection antennae were waving furiously. She had finetuned them in those six months of sabbatical, so determined not to fall into old traps, make old mistakes. Would he share more with her by the end of the day?

'I think you need to travel west of Sydney to see actual last-frontier territory,' she said. 'No kangaroos hopping around the place here.'

'I would like to see kangaroos that aren't in a

zoo,' he said. He turned to face her. 'Living in Sydney must be like living in a resort,' he said.

Gemma tried to see the city she'd lived in all her life through his eyes. It wasn't that she took the beauty of the harbour for granted—it was just that she saw it every day. 'I hadn't thought about it like that but, yes, I see what you mean,' she said. Although she'd worked too hard ever to think she was enjoying a resort lifestyle.

'Do you like living here?' he said.

'Of course,' she said. 'Though I haven't actually lived anywhere else to compare. Sometimes I think I'd like to try a new life in another country. If Party Queens hadn't been such a success, I might have looked for a job as a chef in France. But in the meantime Sydney suits me.'

'I envy you in some ways,' he said. 'Your freedom. The lack of stifling tradition.'

She wondered at the note of yearning in his voice.

'There's a lot more to Sydney than these areas, of course,' she said. 'The Blue Mountains are worth seeing.' She stopped herself from offering to show them to him. He didn't want a tour guide. She didn't want to get too involved. *This was just lunch.*

'I would like to see more, but I go back home on Monday afternoon. With the party on Friday, there is not much time.'

'That's a shame,' she said, keeping her voice light and neutral. She knew this—*Tristan*—was only for today...an interlude. But she already had the feeling that a day, a week, a month wouldn't ever be enough time with him.

'I have responsibilities I must return to.' His tone of voice indicated that he might not be 100 per cent happy about that.

'With your family's corporation? Maybe you could consider opening an Australian branch of the business here,' she said.

He looked ahead of him, and she realised he was purposely not meeting her eyes. 'I'm afraid that is not possible—delightful as the thought might be.'

He turned away from the railing and went over to where he had put down her bag. Again, he pretended it was too heavy to carry, though she could see that with his muscles it must be effortless for him.

'Let's stash your bag somewhere safe and see about that coffee.'

'You don't want to see more sights?'

He paused, her bag held by his side. 'Haven't I

made it clear, Gemma? Forgive my English if I haven't. I've seen a lot of sights in the time I've been in Australia. In the days I have left the only sight I want to see more of is *you*.'

CHAPTER FIVE

TRISTAN SAT OPPOSITE Gemma at a round table inside the cabin. After his second cup of coffee—strong and black—he leaned back in his chair and sighed his satisfaction.

'Excellent coffee, thank you,' he said. Of all the good coffee he'd enjoyed in Australia, he rated this the highest.

Gemma looked pleased. 'We're very fussy about coffee at Party Queens—single origin, fair trade, the best.'

'It shows,' Tristan said.

He liked Party Queens' meticulous attention to detail. It was one of the reasons he felt confident that his reception on Friday would be everything he wanted it to be—although for reasons of security he hadn't shared with them the real nature of the gathering.

'Not true,' Tristan muttered under his breath in his own language. He could have told Eliza by now. The reason he was holding back on the full facts was that he wanted to delay telling Gemma the truth about himself for as long as possible. Things would not be the same once his anonymity was gone.

'I'm glad you like the coffee. How about the food?' she asked.

Her forehead was pleated with the trace of a frown, and he realised she was anxious about his opinion.

'Excellent,' he pronounced. Truth be told, he'd scarcely noticed it. Who would be interested in food when he could feast his eyes on the beautiful woman in front of him?

To please her, he gave his full attention to the superbly arranged fruit platter that included some of the ripe mangoes he had come to enjoy in Queensland. There was also a selection of bite-sized cookies—both savoury, with cheese, and sweet, studded with nuts—arranged on the bottom tier of a silver stand. On the top tier were small square cakes covered in dark chocolate and an extravagant coating of shredded coconut.

'It all looks very good,' he said.

'I know there's more food than we can possibly eat, but we knew nothing about your lunch date and her tastes in food,' Gemma said.

'In that case I hope you chose food *you* liked,' he said.

'As a matter of fact, I did,' she said, with a delightful display of dimples.

'What is this cake with the coconut?' he asked.

'You haven't seen a lamington before?'

He shook his head.

'If Australia had a national cake it would be the lamington,' she said. 'They say it was created in honour of Lord Lamington, a nineteenth-century governor.'

'So this cake has illustrious beginnings?'

'You could call it a grand start for a humble little cake. In this case they are perhaps more illustrious, as I made them using the finest Montovian chocolate.'

'A Montovian embellishment of an Australian tradition?'

'I suspect our traditions are mere babies compared to yours,' she said with another flash of dimples. 'Would you like to try one?'

Tristan bit into a lamington. 'Delicious.'

Truth be told, he preferred lighter food. He had to sit through so many official dinners, with course after rich course, that he ate healthily when he had the choice. The mangoes were more to his taste. But he would not hurt her feelings by telling her so.

Gemma looked longingly at the rest of the cakes. 'I have the world's sweetest tooth—which is a problem in this job. I have to restrict myself to just little tastes of what we cook, or I'd be the size of a house.'

'You're in very good shape,' he said.

She had a fabulous body. Slim, yet with alluring curves. He found it almost impossible to keep his eyes from straying to it. He would have liked to say more about how attractive he found her, but it would not be appropriate. *Not yet...perhaps not ever.*

She flushed high on her cheekbones. 'Thank you. I wasn't fishing for a compliment.'

'I know that,' he said.

The mere fact that she was so unassuming about her beauty made him want to shower her with compliments. To praise the cuteness of her freckles, her sensational curves. To admit to the way he found himself wanting to make her smile just to see her dimples.

There was so much he found pleasing about her. But he was not in a position to express his interest. Gemma wasn't a vacation-fling kind of girl—he'd realised that the moment he met her. And that was all he could ever offer her.

It was getting more difficult by the minute to keep that at the top of his mind.

'I'll try just half a lamington and then some fruit,' she said.

She sliced one into halves with a knife and slowly nibbled on one half with an expression of bliss, her eyes half closed. As she licked a stray shred of coconut from her lovely bow-shaped top lip, she tilted back her head and gave a little moan of pleasure.

Tristan shifted in his seat, gripped the edge of the table so hard it hurt. It was impossible for his thoughts not to stray to speculation about her appetite for other pleasures, to how she would react to his mouth on hers, his touch...

There was still a small strand of coconut at the corner of her mouth. He ached to lean across the table, taste the chocolate on her lips, lick away that stray piece of coconut.

She looked at him through eyes still half narrowed with sensual appreciation. 'The Montovian chocolate makes that the best lamington I've ever tasted.'

She should *always* have chocolate from Montovia.

Tristan cleared his throat. He had to keep their conversation going to distract himself. In his hedonistic past he had been immune to the seduction techniques of worldly, sophisticated temptresses, who knew exactly what they were doing as they tried to snare a prince. Yet the unconscious provocation of this lovely girl eating a piece of cake was making him fall apart.

'I believe you're a trained chef?' he said. 'Tell me how that happened.'

'How I became a chef? Do you really need to know that?'

'I know very little about you. I need to know everything.'

'Oh,' she said, delightfully disconcerted, the flush deepening on her creamy skin. 'If that's what you want...'

'It is what I want,' he said, unable to keep the huskiness from his voice. There was so much more he wanted from her, but it was impossible for him to admit to the desire she was arousing in him.

'Okay,' she said. 'I was always interested in food. My mother wasn't really into cooking and was delighted to let me take over the kitchen whenever I wanted.' She helped herself to some grapes, snipping them from the bunch with a tiny pair of silver scissors.

'So you decided to make a career of it?' It wouldn't be an easy life, he imagined. Hard physical work, as well as particular skills required and—

He completely lost his train of thought. Instead he watched, spellbound, as Gemma popped the fat, purple grapes one by one into her luscious mouth.

Inwardly, he groaned. *This was almost unbearable.*

'Actually, I was all set to be a nutritionist,' she said, seemingly unaware of the torment she was putting him through by the simple act of eating some fruit. 'I started a degree at the University of Newcastle, which is north of Sydney. I stayed up there during the vacations and—'

'Why was that? I went to university in England but came home for at least part of every vacation.'

He'd loved the freedom of living in another country, but home had always been a draw card for him—the security and continuity of the castle, the knowledge of his place in the hierarchy of his country. His parents, who were father and mother to him before they were king and queen.

Gemma pulled a face—which, far from contorting her features, made her look cute. *Had she cast a spell on him?*

'Your home might have been more…welcoming than mine,' she said.

A shadow darkened her warm brown eyes at what was obviously an unpleasant memory. It made him sad for her. His memories of childhood and adolescence were happy. Life at the castle as the 'spare' had been fun—he had had a freedom never granted to his brother. A freedom sorely lost to him now—except for this trip. There had always been some tension between his father and mother, but it had been kept distanced from him. It hadn't been until he'd grown up that he'd discovered the cause of that tension—and why both his parents were so unhappy.

'You were not welcome in your own home?' he asked.

'My mother was always welcoming. My stepfather less so.'

'Was he…abusive?' Tristan tensed, and his hands tightened into fists at the thought of anyone hurting her.

She shook her head. The sunshine slanting in through the windows picked up amber highlights and copper glints in her hair as it fell around her face. He wanted to reach out and stroke it, see if it felt as fiery as it looked.

'Nothing like that,' she said. 'And he wasn't unkind—just indifferent. He didn't want children, but he fell in love with my mother when I was a little kid and I came as part of the package deal.'

'A "package deal"? That seems a harsh way to describe a child.'

Again he felt a surge of protectiveness for her. It was a feeling new to him—this desire to enfold her in safety and shield her from any harm the world might hurl at her. A girl he had known for only a matter of days...

Her shrug of one slender shoulder was obviously an effort to appear nonchalant about an old hurt, but it was not completely successful. 'He couldn't have one without the other. Apparently he wanted my mother badly—she's very beautiful.'

'As is her daughter.' He searched her face. It was disconcerting, the way she seemed to grow lovelier by the minute.

'Thank you.' She flushed again. 'My mother always told me I had to be grateful to my stepfather for looking after us. *Huh.* Even when I was little I looked after myself. But I did my best to please him—to make my mother happy.' She wrinkled her neat, straight nose. 'Why am I telling you all this? I'm sure you must find it boring.'

'You could never be boring, Gemma,' he said. 'I know that about you already.'

It was true. Whether or not she'd cast some kind of witch's spell over him, he found everything about her fascinating. He wanted nothing more than to find out all about her. Just for today, the rest of his life was on hold. It was just him and Gemma, alone in the curious intimacy of a boat in the middle of Sydney Harbour. Like a regular, everyday date of the kind that would not be possible for him once he was back home.

'Are you sure you want to hear more of my ordinary little story?' she asked, her head tilted to one side.

'Nothing could interest me more.'

She could read out loud the list of ingredients from one of her recipes and he'd hang on every word, watching the expressions flit across her face, her dimples peeking in and out. Although so far there didn't appear to be a lot to smile about in her story.

The good-looking dark-haired waiter came to clear their coffee cups and plates. Gemma looked up and smiled at him as she asked him to leave the fruit. Tristan felt a surge of jealousy—until he realised the waiter was more likely to be interested in *him* rather than *her*. Gemma thanked him and praised the chef.

After the waiter had left, she leaned across the table to Tristan. Her voice was lowered to barely above a whisper. 'It feels weird, having people I know serve me,' she said. 'My instinct is to jump up and help. I'm used to being on the other side of the kitchen door.'

Tristan had been used to people serving him since he was a baby. An army of staff catered to the royal family's every need. He'd long ago got used to the presence of servants in the room—so much that they'd become almost invisible. When he went back he would have a hand-picked private staff of his own to help him assume his new responsibilities as crown prince.

The downside was that there was very little privacy. Since his brother had died every aspect of his life had been under constant, intense scrutiny.

Gemma returned to her story. 'Inevitably, when I was a teenager I clashed with my stepfather. It made my mother unhappy. I was glad to leave home for uni—and I never went back except for fleeting visits.'

'And your father?'

'You mean my birth father?'

'Yes.'

'He died before I was born.' Her voice betrayed no emotion. It was as if she were speaking about a stranger.

'That was a tragedy.'

'For my mother, yes. She was a ski instructor in the French resort of Val d'Isère, taking a gap year. My father was English—also a ski instructor. They fell madly in love, she got pregnant, they got married and soon after he got killed in an avalanche.'

'I'm sorry—that's a terrible story.'

Skiing was one of the risky sports he loved, along with mountaineering and skydiving. The castle staff was doing everything it could to wean him off those adrenaline-pumping pastimes. He knew he had to acquiesce. The continuity of the royal family was paramount. His country had lost one heir to an accident and could not afford to lose him, too.

But he railed against being cosseted. Hated having his independence and choice taken away from him. Sometimes the price of becoming king in future seemed unbearably high. But duty over-ruled everything. Tragedy had forced fate's hand. He accepted his inheritance and everything that went with it—no matter the cost to him. *He was now the crown prince.*

Gemma made a dismissive gesture with her hands. 'I didn't know my father, so of course I never missed him. But he was the love of my mother's life. She was devastated. Then his posh parents arrived at the resort, looked down their noses at my mother, questioned the legality of my parents' marriage—it *was* totally legit, by the way—and paid her to forget she was ever married and to never make a claim on them. They even tried to bar her from the funeral back in England.' Her voice rose with indignation.

'You sound angry,' he said. But what her father's parents had done was something *his* parents had done when he and his brother were younger. They would have paid any amount of money to rid the family of an unsuitable woman. Someone who might reflect badly on the throne. A commoner. *Someone like Gemma.*

His parents' actions had slammed home the fact

that marriage for a Montovian prince had nothing to do with love or passion. It was about tradition and duty and strategic alliance. When he had discovered the deep hypocrisy of his parents' relationship, his cynicism about the institution of marriage—or at least how it existed in Montovia—had been born.

That cynicism had only been reinforced by his brother's marriage to the daughter of a duke. The castle had trumpeted it as a 'love match'. Indeed, Carl had been grateful to have found such a pretty, vivacious bride as Sylvie. Only after the splendid wedding in the cathedral had she revealed her true self—venal and avaricious and greedy for the wealth and status that came with being a Montovian princess. She'd cared more for extravagant jewellery than she had for his brother.

Consequently, Tristan had avoided marriage and any attempts to get him to the altar.

He schooled his face to appear neutral, not to give Gemma any indication of what he was thinking. Her flushed face made it very clear that she would *not* be sympathetic to those kind of regal machinations.

'You're darn right. I get angry on behalf of my poor mother—young and grieving,' she said. 'She wanted to throw the money in their faces, but she was carrying me. She swallowed her pride and took the money—for my sake. I was born in London, then she brought me home to Sydney. She said her biggest revenge for their treatment of her was that they never knew they had a grandchild.'

Tristan frowned. He was part of a royal family with a lineage that stretched back hundreds of years. Blood meant everything. 'How did you feel about that?'

Gemma toyed with the remainder of the grapes. He noticed her hands were nicked with little scars and her nails were cut short and unpolished. There were risks in everything—even cooking.

'Of course, I've always felt curious about my English family,' she said. 'I look nothing like my mother or her side of the family. When I was having disagreements with my stepfather, I'd dream of running away to find my other family. I know who they are. But out of loyalty to my mother I've never made any attempt to contact my Clifford relatives.'

'So your name is really Gemma Clifford?'

She shook her head. 'My stepfather adopted me. Legally I bear his name. And that's okay. For all his faults, he gave me a home and supported me.'

'Until you went to university in Newcastle?'

'Whatever his other faults, he's not mean. He kept on paying me an allowance. But I wanted to be independent—free of him and of having to pretend to be someone I was not simply to please him. I talked my way into a part-time kitchen hand's job at the best restaurant in the area. As luck would have it, the head chef was an incredibly talented young guy. He became a culinary superstar in Europe in the years that followed. Somehow he saw talent in me and offered me an apprenticeship as a chef. I didn't hesitate to ditch my degree and accept—much to my parents' horror. But it was what I really wanted to do.'

'Have you ever regretted it?'

'Not for a minute.'

'It seems a big jump from chef to co-owning Party Queens,' Tristan said.

Gemma offered the remaining grapes to him. When he refused, she popped some more into her mouth. He waited for her to finish them.

'It's a roundabout story. When my boss left for grander culinary pastures, his replacement wasn't so encouraging of me. I left the Newcastle restaurant and went back to Sydney.'

'To work in restaurants?'

'Yes—some very good ones. But it's still a very male-dominated industry. Most of the top chefs are men. Females like me only too often get relegated to being pastry chefs and are passed over for promotion. I got sick of the bullying in the kitchen. The sexist behaviour. I got the opportunity to work on a glossy women's magazine as an assistant to the food editor and grabbed it. In time I became a food editor myself, and my career took off.'

'That still doesn't explain Party Queens,' he said. 'Seems to me there's a gap there.' He'd trained as a lawyer. He was used to seeing what was missing from an argument, what lay beneath a story.

She leaned across the table and rested on her elbows. 'Are you interviewing me?' Her words were playful, but her eyes were serious.

'Of course not. I'm just interested. You're very successful. I want to know how you got there.'

'I've worked hard—be in no doubt about that. But luck plays a part in it, too.'

'It always does,' he said.

Lucky he had walked in on her in her kitchen. Lucky he'd been born into a royal family. And yet there were days when he resented that lucky accident of birth. Like right here, right now, spending time with this woman, knowing that he could not take this attraction, which to his intense gratification appeared to be mutual, *anywhere*. Because duty to his country required sacrificing his own desires.

'There's bad luck too, of course,' Gemma went on. 'Andie was lifestyle editor on the magazine— she'd trained as an interior designer. Eliza was on the publishing side. We became friends. Then the magazine closed without warning and we were all suddenly without a job.'

'That must have been a blow,' he said. He had never actually worked for an employer, apart from his time as a conscript in the Montovian military. His 'job prospects'—short of an exceedingly unlikely revolution—were assured for life.

Again, Gemma shrugged one slender shoulder. 'It happens in publishing. We rolled with it.'

'I can see that,' he said. He realised how resilient she was. And independent. She got more appealing by the minute.

'People asked us to organise parties for them while we were looking for other jobs—between us we had all the skills. The party bookings grew, and we began to see we had a viable business.

That's how Party Queens was born. We never dreamed it would become as successful as it has.'

'I'm impressed. With you and with your business. With all this.' He indicated the *Argus*, the harbour, the meal.

'We aim to please,' she said with that bewitching smile.

He could imagine only too well how she might please him and he her.

But he was not here in Sydney to make impossible promises to a girl next door like Gemma. Nor did he want to seduce her with lies just for momentary physical thrills.

Or to put his own heart at any kind of risk.

This could be for only one day.

CHAPTER SIX

GEMMA COULDN'T REMEMBER when she'd last felt so at ease with a man. So utterly comfortable in his presence. Had she *ever* before felt like this?

But she didn't want to question the *why* of it. Just to enjoy his company while she had the chance.

After she'd polished off all the grapes, she and Tristan had moved back out onto the deck. He hadn't eaten much—no more cake and just some mango. She'd got the impression he was very disciplined in his eating habits—and probably everything else. But getting to know Tristan was still very much a guessing game.

The *Argus* had left the inner harbour behind and set course north for Manly and their lunchtime destination of Store Beach. The sun had moved around since they'd gone inside for coffee, and the crew had moved two vintage steamer-style wooden deckchairs into the shade, positioned to take advantage of the view.

She adjusted the cushions, which were printed

with anchor motifs, and settled down into one of them. Tristan was to her right, with a small table between them. But as soon as she'd sat down, she moved to get up again.

'My hat,' she explained. 'I need to get it from my bag. Even though we're in the shade, I could get burned.'

Immediately, Tristan was on his feet. 'Let me get it for you,' he said, ushering her to sit back down.

'There's no need. Please… I can do it,' she protested.

'I insist,' he said in a tone that brooked no further resistance.

Gemma went to protest again, then realised that would sound ungracious. *She wasn't used to being cared for by a man.* 'Thank you,' she conceded. 'It's right at the top of the bag.'

'Next to the rolling pins?' he said.

'But no wooden spoons,' she said with a smile.

Not only would Alistair not have dreamed of fetching her hat for her, he would have demanded she get him a beer while she was up. *Good manners were very appealing in a man.*

Tristan held himself with a mix of upright bearing and athletic grace as he headed back into the cabin. Gemma lay back and watched him through her sunglasses. His back view was every bit as pleasing as his front. Broad shoulders tapered to a wide back and then narrow hips. *There could be no doubt that a good butt was also an asset in a man.*

He looked effortlessly classy in the white linen trousers and the loose white shirt. They were so perfectly cut she wondered if they'd been tailored to fit him. Could you get men's casual clothes made to measure? She knew you could have suits bespoke. Anything was possible if you had enough money, she supposed.

He returned with her hat—a favourite white panama. She reached out to take it from him, but he came to the side of her chair and bent down to put it on her head. His face was very close. She could almost imagine he was bending down to kiss her. If he did, she wouldn't stop him. No... she might even kiss him first. She was thankful her sunglasses masked her eyes, so her expression didn't give her away.

'Nice hat,' he said as he placed it on her head. As he tugged it into place, his hands strayed lightly over her hair, her ears, her throat—just the merest touch, but it was enough to set her trembling.

She forced her voice to sound steady—not to betray how excitingly unnerving she found his nearness. 'I've had this hat for years, and I would be greatly distressed if I lost it.'

Again she caught his scent. She remembered how years ago in high school she'd dated a perfectly nice boy who'd had everything going for him, but she hadn't liked the way he'd smelled. Not that he'd been unclean or unwashed—it was just his natural scent that had turned her off. But Tristan's fresh scent sent her nerve endings into a flurry of awareness.

Was there *anything* about Tristan she didn't find appealing?

His underlying mystery, that sense of him holding back still had her guard up—but perhaps that mystery was part of his appeal. And it was in her power to find out what made Tristan tick. *Just ask him, Gemma.*

There were many points of interest she could draw his attention to on their way to Manly. But she would not waste time on further guidebook lectures. *The only sight I want to see more of is you,* he'd said.

Did he have any idea of how good those words made her feel?

Her self-esteem had taken a terrible battering from Alistair. Six months had not been enough to fix it fully. Just hours in Tristan's company had her feeling better about herself than she had for a long time. The insistent twitching of her antennae told her that his charming words might be calculated to disarm and seduce. But her deeper instincts sensed sincerity—though for what purpose she was still at a loss.

Enjoy the moment, she told herself, *because that's all you've got with him.*

After Tristan had settled into his deckchair, she turned to him, slipped off her sunglasses. 'Your interview technique is so good you know quite a lot about me. Now it's my turn to discover Tristan.'

He gestured with his hands to indicate emptiness. 'There is not much I can tell you,' he said.

Did he mean that literally?

For all the instant intimacy of the situation, she still sensed those secrets. Her antennae waved gently, to remind her to be wary of men who were not what they seemed.

'Ask me questions—I will see if I can answer them,' he said.

As in, he would see if he was *able* to answer

her questions? Or *allowed* to answer them? Or he just plain didn't *want* to answer them?

She chose her first question with care. 'What language do you speak in Montovia?' she asked. 'French? German? I think I can detect both in your accent.'

'We speak Montovian—our own language,' he said. 'We are a small country and it is influenced by the other European countries that surround us.'

'Say something to me in Montovian,' she said. 'I'm interested in languages.'

'I've been told it is not an attractive language, so I am warning you,' he said. 'Even to my ears it sounds quite harsh.'

He turned to her and spoke a few sentences as he gazed into her eyes. She tried to ignore the way his proximity made her heart race.

'I didn't understand a word of that, but your language is not unattractive.' And neither was his voice—deep, masculine, arresting. 'What did you actually say to me?'

'You really want to know?'

'Yes.'

'I said that the beauty of this magnificent harbour could not compare to the beauty of the woman sitting beside me.'

Spoken by anyone else, the words might have sounded corny, over the top. But spoken with Tristan's accent they were swoon worthy.

'Oh,' she said, again lost for words. She felt herself blush—that was the problem with being a creamy-skinned redhead...there was no hiding her reactions. 'Seriously?'

He smiled. 'You'll never know, will you? Unless you learn Montovian—and no one outside of my country learns Montovian.'

'Why not?'

'Because it is only spoken in Montovia. I also speak German, French, Italian and Spanish,' he said.

'I'm seriously impressed,' she said. 'I studied French and Italian at school. Then German at night school before I went to Europe on a backpackers' bus tour. But I never use those languages here, and I fear I've lost what skills I had.'

'You'd pick them up again in the right environment. I was out of the habit of speaking English, but I'm getting better at it every day.' His eyes narrowed in that intense way he had of looking at her, as if he were seeking answers—to what, she didn't know. 'Especially talking to you, Gemma'.

'You've inspired me to study some more so that—'

Only just in time she caught herself from saying, *So that next time I'll surprise you by speaking fluent French.* She was surprised at the sharp twist of pain at the reminder that there would be no next time for her and Tristan.

She finished her sentence, hoping he hadn't noticed the pause. 'So that my skills don't just dwindle away. Did you learn English at school?'

'Yes. I also had a tutor. My parents felt it was essential we spoke good English.'

'"We"? You have brothers and sisters?'

Tristan stared out to sea. 'I have a younger sister. I...I had an older brother. He...he died when his helicopter came down in the mountains a year ago.'

Gemma wasn't sure what to say that wouldn't be a cliché. 'I...I'm so sorry to hear that,' was the best she could manage.

His jaw tightened. 'It was...terrible. His wife and their little boy were with him. My family will never get over it.'

Gemma was too shocked to speak. She went to reach out and put her hand on his arm but decided against it, not sure how welcome her touch would be in this moment of remembered tragedy.

'I carry the loss of my brother with me in my heart. There is not a day that I do not think of him.'

'I'm so sorry,' she said again. She wished she could give him comfort. But they were still essentially strangers.

He took a deep breath. 'But enough of sadness,' he said. He turned to her. 'I don't want to talk about tragic things, Gemma.'

There was a bleakness in his eyes, and his face seemed shadowed. She was an only child. She couldn't imagine how it would feel to lose a sibling—*and* his sibling's family. 'No,' she agreed.

How lucky she'd been in her life not to have suffered tragedy. The loss of her birth father hadn't really touched her, though she suspected her mother still secretly grieved. Gemma *had* had her share of heartbreak, though. She had genuinely loved Alistair, and the way their relationship had ended had scarred her—perhaps irredeemably. It would be difficult to trust again.

A silence fell between them that Gemma didn't know quite how to fill. 'Tell me more about Montovia,' she said eventually. 'Are there magnificent old buildings? Do you have lots of winter sports? Do you have a national costume?'

'Yes to all of that. Montovia is very beautiful and traditional. It has many medieval buildings. There is also a modern administrative capital, where the banks and financial services are situated.'

'And the chocolate?'

'The so-important chocolate? It is made in a charming old factory building near the lake, which is a tourist attraction in its own right.'

I'd love to go there some day.

Her words hung unspoken in the air between them. Never could she utter them. He was a tourist—just passing through before he went back to his own life. And she was a woman guarding her heart against falling for someone impossible.

'That sounds delightful,' she said.

'There is a wonderful chocolate shop and tea room near my home. I used to love to go there when I was a child. So...so did my brother and sister.'

Gemma wondered about his sister, but didn't want to ask. 'Where do you live?' she said instead.

He took another deep breath. It seemed to Gemma that he needed to steady himself against unhappy thoughts. His brother must be entwined in Tristan's every childhood memory.

'I live in the old capital of Montovia—which is also called Montovia.'

'That could get confusing, couldn't it?'

'Everyone knows it. The town of Montovia grew up around the medieval castle and the cathedral and sits on the edge of a lake.'

Gemma sat forward in her chair. 'A castle? You live near a *castle*?'

'But of course. Montovia is ruled by a hereditary monarchy.'

'You mean a king and a queen?'

'Yes.'

'I wasn't expecting that. I assumed Montovia would be a republic—a democracy.'

'It is... We have a hereditary monarchy, but also a representative democracy with an elected parliament—and a legal system, of course.'

'So the king and queen are figureheads?'

He shook his head. 'They are rulers, with the power to dissolve parliament. Although that has never happened.'

'Castles and kings and queens—it sounds like something out of a fairytale.' She was too polite to say it sounded feudalistic. Not when he sounded so passionate, defending a way of life that didn't seem of this century.

'On the contrary, it is very real. Our country is prosperous. Montovians are very patriotic. Each of our subjects—I…uh…I mean the people…would fight to the death to protect their way of life. We have compulsory military service to ensure we are ready in case they should ever have to.'

'You mean conscription?'

'Yes. For all males aged eighteen. Women can volunteer, and many do.'

She shuddered. 'I don't think I would want to do that.'

'They would probably welcome someone like you as a cook.'

He smiled. Was he teasing her?

'But I'd still have to do the military training. I've seen what soldiers have to do—running with big packs on their back, obstacle courses, weapons…' Her voice dwindled away at the sheer horror of even contemplating it.

'Sign up even as a cook and you'd have to do the training. And no wooden spoons as weapons.'

'You'll never let me forget that, will you?'

'Never,' he said, his smile widening into a grin.

Until he went on his way and never gave this girl in Sydney another thought.

Why were they even talking about this? She was unlikely to visit Montovia, let alone sign up for its military.

'Did you serve?' she asked.

'Of course. My time in the army was one of the best times of my life.'

Oh, yes. She could imagine him in uniform. With his broad shoulders and athletic build. That must be where his bearing came from. Tristan in uniform would be even hotter than Tristan in casual clothes. Or Tristan without any—

Don't go there, Gemma.

But her curiosity about Montovia was piqued. When she went home this evening, she would look up the country and its customs on the internet.

'Did you actually have to go to battle?' she asked.

'I spent time with the peacekeeping forces in eastern Europe. My brother went to Africa. It was good for us to see outside our own protected world.'

'You know, I wasn't really aware that such kingdoms as Montovia still existed.'

'Our royal family has ruled for centuries,' he

said—rather stiffly, she thought. 'The people love the royal family of Montovia.'

'Do *you*?' she asked. 'You're not harbouring any secret republican leanings?'

His eyebrows rose, and he looked affronted. 'Never. I am utterly loyal to the king and queen. My country would not be Montovia without the royal family and our customs and traditions.'

Gemma was silent for a long moment. 'It's all so outside of my experience. As a child I led an everyday suburban existence in a middle-class suburb of Sydney. You grew up in a town with a medieval castle ruled by a king and queen. What...what different lives we must lead.'

He steepled his fingers together. 'Yes. Very different.'

Tristan was glad of the interruption when the waiter brought out a tray with the cool drinks they had ordered. *He had to be more careful.* He'd been on tenterhooks while chatting with Gemma for fear that he would inadvertently reveal the truth about himself and his family. There had been a few minor slip-ups, but nothing that couldn't be excused as a mistake with his English.

He drank iced tea as Gemma sipped on diet cola. It was too early for anything stronger.

The longer he maintained this deception, the harder it would become to confess to it. But did that really matter? After the party on Friday night he wouldn't need to be in any further contact with Party Queens. Or with Gemma.

He could leave the reveal until she found out for herself—when he appeared at his party wearing his ceremonial sash and medals. No doubt she would be shocked, would maybe despise him for lying to her. Her opinion should not matter—he would never see her again after the party.

But her opinion of him did matter. *It mattered very much.*

Just now there had been an opportunity for him to explain his role in the royal family of Montovia—but he had not been able to bring himself to take it. He was still hanging on fiercely to the novelty of being just Tristan in Gemma's eyes.

'I haven't finished my interrogation yet,' she said, a playful smile lifting the corners of her mouth.

He liked it that she was unaware of his wealth and status. It must be obvious to her that he was rich. But she seemed more interested in *him* than in what he had. It was refreshing.

'You said you went to university in England?' she asked.

'To Cambridge—to study European law.'

Her finely arched auburn brows rose. 'You're a lawyer?'

'I don't actually practise as a lawyer. I have always worked for…for my family's business. A knowledge of European law is necessary.'

For trade. For treaties. For the delicate negotiations required by a small country that relied in some measure on the goodwill of surrounding countries—but never took that goodwill for granted.

'Is it your father's business?'

'Yes. And it was my grandparents' before that.' Back and back and back, in an unbroken chain of Montovia's hereditary monarchy. It had been set to continue in his brother's hands—not his.

Tristan knew he could not avoid talking about his brother, much as it still hurt. There'd been an extravagance of public mourning for his brother's death—and the death of his little son, whose birth had placed a second male between Tristan and the throne. But with all the concern about his unexpected succession to the position of crown prince, Tristan hadn't really been able to mourn the loss of Carl, his brother and best friend. Not Carl the crown prince. And his sweet little nephew. This trip away had been part of that grieving process. Being with Gemma was helping.

'My brother played a senior role in the…the business. I now have to step up to take his role.'

'And you're not one hundred per cent happy about that, are you?'

'I never anticipated I would have to do it. The job is not my choice.'

Not only had he loved his brother, he had also admired the way Carl had handled the role of crown prince. Tristan had never resented not being the heir. He had never been sure if he had an unquestioning allegiance to the old ways in order not to challenge the archaic rules that restricted the royal family's existence even in the twenty-first century. One onerous rule in particular…

'Will it bring more responsibility?' Gemma asked. 'Will you be more involved in the chocolate side of things?'

For a moment he wasn't sure what she meant.

Then he remembered how he had deliberately implied that chocolate was part of his family's business.

'More the finance and managerial side,' he said. And everything else it took to rule the country.

'I'm sure you will rise to the challenge and do a wonderful job,' she said.

He frowned. 'Why do you say that, Gemma, when we scarcely know each other?'

Her eyes widened. 'Even in this short time I'm convinced of your integrity,' she said. 'I believe you will want to honour your brother's memory by doing the best job you can.'

His integrity. Short of downright lying, he had been nothing but evasive about who he was from the moment they'd met. How would she react when she found out the truth?

The longer he left it, the worse it would be.

He turned to face her. 'Gemma, I—'

Gemma suddenly got up from her deckchair, clutching her hat to her head against a sudden gust of wind. 'We're passing across the Heads.'

'The Heads?'

'It's the entrance from the ocean to Sydney Harbour, guarded by two big headlands—North

Head and South Head. But, being exposed to the
Pacific Ocean, the sea can get rough here, so prepare for a rocky ride ahead.'

CHAPTER SEVEN

TRISTAN HAD PLANNED with military precision in order to make this day with Gemma happen. But one important detail had escaped his plan.

He cursed his inattention with a blast of favourite curse words. Both relatively sheltered when they'd been conscripted to the military, he and his brother had expanded their vocabulary of new and interesting words with great glee. He had never lost the skill.

Gemma was standing beside him at the bow of the *Argus*. 'Do I detect some choice swearing in Montovian?' she asked with a teasing smile.

'Yes,' he said, still furious with himself.

'Can you translate for me?'

'No,' he said.

'Or tell me what it was all about?'

Exasperated, he waved his hand to encompass the view. 'Look at this place—Store Beach...even more perfect than you said it would be.'

'And there's a problem with that?'

The *Argus* had dropped anchor some one hundred metres from shore. The beach was more what he would call a bay, with a sheltered, curving stretch of golden sand. Eucalypt trees and other indigenous plants grew right down to where the sand started. The water rippled through shades of azure to wash up on the beach in a lacy white froth. The air was tangy with salt and the sharp scent of the eucalypts. It took no stretch of the imagination to feel as if they were on a remote island somewhere far away.

'Not a problem with the beach,' he said. 'It's difficult to believe such a pristine spot could be so close to a major city.'

'That's why we chose Store Beach for your lunch date,' she said. 'And, being midweek, we've got it all to ourselves. So what's the problem?'

'It's hot, the water looks awesome, I want to swim. But I didn't think to bring a swimsuit—or order one for you.'

Her eyebrows rose. 'For me? *Order* a swimsuit for me?'

'Of course. You would not have known to bring one as you thought you would be working. There is a concierge at my hotel—I should have asked her to purchase a choice of swimsuits for you.'

Gemma's brows drew together in a frown. 'Are you serious?'

'But of course.'

'You are, aren't you?' Her voice was underscored with incredulity.

'Is there something wrong with that?'

'Nothing *wrong*, I guess. But it's not the kind of thing an Australian guy would do, that's for sure. None that *I* know, anyway.'

Tristan realised he might sound arrogant, but went ahead anyway. 'It is the kind of thing I would do, and I am annoyed that I did not do so.'

She tilted her head to one side, observing him as if he were an object of curiosity. 'How would you have known my size?'

'I have observed your figure.' He couldn't help but cast an appreciative eye over the curves of her breasts and hips, her trim waist. 'I would have made a very good estimate.'

Immediately, he suspected he might have said the wrong thing. Again he muttered a Montovian curse. Under stress—and the way she was looking at him *was* making him stressed—he found his English wasn't turning out quite the way he wanted it to.

Thankfully, after a stunned silence on her part,

Gemma erupted into a peal of delightful laughter. 'Okay…I'm flattered you've made such a close observation of my figure.'

'It's not that I…I didn't mean—'

Her voice was warm with laughter. 'I think I know what you mean.'

'I did not say something…inappropriate?'

'You kinda did—but let's put it down to culture clash.'

'You do not think me…bad mannered? Rude?'

Crass. That was the word he was seeking. It was at the tip of his tongue. He had a master's degree in law from a leading English university. Why were his English language skills deserting him?

It was *her.*

Gemma.

Since the moment she'd come at him with her wooden spoon and pink oven mitts she'd had him—what was the word?—*discombobulated.* He was proud he had found the correct, very difficult English word, but why didn't he feel confident about pronouncing it correctly? The way she made him feel had him disconcerted, disorientated, behaving in ways he knew he should not.

But the way she was smiling up at him, with her dimples and humour in her brown eyes, made him feel something else altogether. *Something that was forbidden for him to feel for a commoner.*

She stretched up on her toes to kiss him lightly on the cheek, as she had done when she'd boarded the boat. This time her lips lingered longer, and she was so close he inhaled her heady scent of vanilla and lemon and a hint of chocolate, felt the warmth of her body. He put his hand to his cheek, where he had felt the soft tenderness of her lips, and held it there for a moment too long.

'I don't think you're at all rude,' she said. 'I think you're charming and funny and generous... and I...I...'

For a long moment her gaze held his, and the flush high on her cheekbones deepened. Tristan held his breath, on tenterhooks over what she might say next. But she took a step back, took a deep, steadying breath—which made her breasts rise enticingly under her snug-fitting top—and said something altogether different from what he'd hoped she might say.

'And I can solve your swimsuit problem for you,' she said.

'You can?'

'First the problem of a swimsuit for me. That impossibly big bag of mine also contains a swimsuit and towel. The North Sydney Olympic Pool is on the way from Lavender Bay wharf to my apartment in Kirribilli. I intended to swim there on my way home—as I often do.'

'That's excellent—so you at least can dive in and swim.'

'So can you.'

'But I—'

'I understand if you don't want to go in salt water in your smart white trousers. Or…or in your underwear.'

Her voice had faltered when she'd mentioned his underwear. A sudden image of her in *her* underwear flashed through his mind—lovely Gemma, swimming in lacy sheer bra and panties, her auburn hair streaming behind her in the water…

He had to clear his throat to speak. 'So what do you suggest?'

'In a closet in the stateroom is a selection of brand-new swimwear for both men and women. Choose a swimsuit and the cost of it will be added to the boat hire invoice.'

'Perfect,' he said. 'You get everything right, don't you, Party Queen Gemma?'

Her expression dimmed. 'Perhaps not everything. But I'll claim this one.'

'Shall we go swimming?' he asked. 'I saw a swimming platform aft on the boat.' His skin prickled with heat. He should have worn shorts and a T-shirt instead of trying to impress Gemma in his bespoke Italian sportswear. 'I can't wait to get into that water.'

'Me, too. I can't think of anything I would rather do on a beautiful day like this.'

Tristan could think of a number of things he'd like to do with *her* on a beautiful day like this. All of which involved them wearing very few clothes—if any at all.

Gemma changed quickly and went back out onto the deck, near the swimming platform at the back. Tristan had gone into the stateroom to choose a swimsuit and change. She felt inexplicably shy as she waited for him. Although she swam often, she never felt 100 per cent comfortable in a swimsuit. The occupational hazard of a career filled with tempting food made her always think she needed to lose a few pounds to look her best in Lycra.

Her swimsuit was a modest navy racer-back one-piece, with contrast panels of aqua and white down the sides. More practical than glamorous.

Not, in fact, the slightest bit seductive. Which was probably as well…

The door from the stateroom opened and Tristan headed towards her. Tristan had confessed to 'observing' her body. She smiled at the thought of his flustered yet flattering words. She straightened her shoulders and sucked in her tummy. And then immediately sucked in a breath as well at the sight of him. He'd looked good in his clothes, but without them—well, *nearly* without them—he was breathtaking in his masculinity.

Wearing stylish swim shorts in a tiny dark-blue-and-purple check and nothing else, he strode towards her with athletic grace and a complete lack of self-consciousness. *He was gorgeous.* Those broad shoulders, the defined muscles of his chest and arms, the classic six-pack belly and long, leanly muscled legs were in perfect proportion. He didn't have much body hair—just a dusting in the right places, set off against smooth golden skin.

He smiled his appreciation of *her* in a swimsuit. His smile and those vivid blue eyes, his handsome, handsome face and the warmth of his expression directed at her, all made her knees so wobbly she had to hold on to the deck railing for support. Her antennae didn't just wave frantically—they set off tiny, shrill alarms.

She realised she was holding her breath, and it came out as a gasp she had to disguise as a cough.

'Are you okay?' Tristan asked.

'F-fine,' she said as soon as she was able to recover her voice. As fine as a red-blooded woman *could* be when faced with a vision of such masculine perfection and trying to pretend she wasn't affected.

The crew had left a stack of red-and-white-striped beach towels in a basket on the deck. Tristan picked one up and handed it to her. 'Your swimsuit is very smart,' he said.

The open admiration in his eyes when he looked at her made her decide she had no cause for concern about what he thought of her shape.

She had to clear her throat. 'So…so is yours.'

Tristan picked up a towel for himself and slung it around his neck. As he did so, Gemma noticed something that marred all that physical perfection—a long, reddish scar that stretched along the top of his shoulder.

Tristan must have noticed the line of her gaze. 'You have observed my battle wound?'

She frowned. 'I thought you said you didn't go to war?'

'I mean my battle wound from the polo field. I came off one of my ponies and smashed my collarbone.'

She wanted to lean over and stroke it but didn't. 'Ouch. That must have hurt.'

'Yes. It did,' he said with understatement.

She didn't know if it was Tristan's way or just the way he spoke English. She wondered how different he might be if she were able to converse with him in fluent Montovian.

'I have a titanium plate and eight pins in it.'

'And your pony?' Gemma wasn't much of a horseback rider, but she knew that what was called a polo 'pony' was actually a very expensive and highly trained thoroughbred horse. Polo was a sport for the very wealthy.

'He was not hurt, thank heaven—he is my favourite pony. We have won many chukkas together.'

'Can you still play polo?'

'I hope to be able to play in the Montovian team this summer.'

She could imagine Tristan in the very tight white breeches and high black boots of a polo player, fearlessly ducking and weaving in perfect unison with a magnificent horse.

'You play polo for your country?'

'I have that honour, yes,' he said.

Again she got that feeling of *otherness*. Not only did he and she come from different countries and cultures, it seemed Tristan came from a different side of the tracks, as well. The posh, extremely wealthy side. Her stepfather was hardly poor, but he was not wealthy in the way she suspected Tristan was wealthy. Dennis was an orthodontist, with several lucrative practices. She could thank him for her perfectly aligned teeth and comfortable middle-class upbringing.

As a single mother, I could never have given you this life, her mother had used to say, reinforcing her instructions for Gemma always to be grateful and acquiescent. *Why couldn't you have married someone who didn't always make me feel in the way?* Gemma had wanted to shout back. But she had loved her mother too much to rebel.

Running a string of polo ponies, hiring a luxury yacht on Sydney Harbour for just two people, the upcoming no-expenses-spared function on Friday night all seemed to speak of a very healthy income. If she thought about it, Tristan had actually *bought* her company on the boat today—and it had been a very expensive purchase.

But she didn't care about any of that.

She liked Tristan—*really* liked him—and he was far and away the most attractive man she had ever met. It was a waste of time to worry when she just wanted to enjoy his company.

She reached into her outsize bag for her high-protection sunscreen. 'You go in the water. I still have to put on some sun protection,' she said to Tristan.

'I'll wait for you,' he said.

Aware of Tristan's intense gaze, she felt self-conscious smoothing cream over her arms and legs, then twisting and turning to get to the spot on her back she could never quite reach. 'Australia is probably not the best climate for me,' she said. 'I burn, I blister, I freckle...'

'I think your pale skin is lovely,' he said. 'Don't try to tan it.'

'Thank you,' she said. It wasn't a compliment she heard often in a country obsessed with tanning.

'Let me help,' said Tristan. He grabbed the

tube of sunscreen before she could protest. 'Turn around.'

She tensed as she heard him fling the towel from around his neck, squeeze cream from the tube. Then relaxed as she felt his hands on her back, slowly massaging in the cream with strong, sure fingers, smoothing it across her shoulders and down her arms in firm, sweeping motions.

The sensation of his hands on her body was utter bliss—she felt as if she was melting under his touch. When his hands slid down her back, they traced the sides of her breasts, and her nipples tightened. His breath fanned her hair, warm and intimate. She closed her eyes and gave herself over to sensation. *To Tristan.*

Her breathing quickened as her body responded to him, and from behind her she heard his breath grow ragged. He rested his hands on her waist. She twisted around, her skin slick with cream, and found herself in the circle of his arms.

For a long, silent moment she looked up into his face—already familiar, dangerously appealing. She knew he would see in her eyes the same mix of yearning and desire and wariness she saw in his: the same longing for something she knew was unwise. She swayed towards him as he lowered his head and splayed her hands against his bare, hard chest, his warm skin. She sighed as his lips touched hers in the lightest of caresses, pressed her mouth against his as she returned his kiss.

He murmured against her mouth. 'Gemma, I—'

Then another voice intruded. 'Gemma, I need to get your opinion on the plating of the yellow-tail kingfish *carpaccio*. Do you want— Oh. *Sorry*. I didn't realise I was interrupting—'

Gemma broke away from Tristan's kiss. Glared over his shoulder to her chef, who had his hands up in surrender as he backed away.

'No need. I'll sort the *carpaccio* out for myself.'

But he had a big grin plastered on his face, and she knew the team at Party Queens would find out very soon that Gemma had been caught kissing the client. She muttered a curse in English— one she was sure Tristan would understand. *She wanted to keep Tristan to herself.*

Tristan's arms remained firmly around her, and she didn't really want to leave them. But when he pulled her towards him again, she resisted. 'It's as well our chef came along,' she said. 'We shouldn't really be starting something we can't continue, should we?'

Tristan cleared his throat, but his voice was husky when he replied. 'You are right—we should not. But that does not stop me wanting to kiss you.'

She took a step back. 'Me neither. I mean I want to kiss *you*, too. But...but you're only here a few days and I—'

I'm in danger of falling for you, even though I hardly know you and I have to protect myself from the kind of pain that could derail me.

'I understand. It would be best for both of us.' He sounded as if he spoke through gritted teeth.

Disappointment flooded through her but also relief that he hadn't pressed for more. After the world of promise in that brief, tender kiss, she might have been tempted to ignore those frantically waving antennae and throw away every self-protective measure and resolve she had made in that lonely six months.

'Yes,' was all she could murmur from a suddenly choked throat.

'What I really need is to get into that cold water,' he said.

'You mean...like a cold shower?'

'Yes,' he said, more grimly than she had heard him speak before.

'Me, too,' she said.

He held out his hand. 'Are you coming with me?'

CHAPTER EIGHT

AS TRISTAN SWAM alongside Gemma, seeing her pale limbs and the auburn hair floating around her shoulders reminded him of the Montovian myths of water nymphs. Legend had it that these other-world temptresses in human form inhabited the furthest reaches of the vast lakes of Montovia. They were young, exquisite and shunned human contact.

If a man were to come across such a nymph, he would instantly become besotted, bewitched, obsessed by her. His beautiful nymph would entice him to make love to her until he was too exhausted to swim and he'd drown—still in her embrace—in the deepest, coldest waters. The rare man who survived and found his way home would go mad with grief and spend the rest of his life hunting the shores of the lakes in a desperate effort to find his nymph again.

Montovians were a deeply superstitious people—even the most well educated and sophisticated of them. Tristan shrugged off those ancient myths, but in a small part of his soul they lived on despite his efforts to deny them.

Gemma swam ahead of him with effortless, graceful strokes, ducking beneath the water, turning and twisting her body around. How did he describe how she seemed in the water? *Joyous.* That was the word. She was quite literally in her element, playing in the water like some...well, like a nymph enchantress.

She turned back to face him, her hair slicked back off her face, revealing her fine bone structure, the scattering of freckles across the bridge of her nose. She trod water until he caught up with her.

'Isn't the water wonderful?' she said. 'I would have hated you if I'd had to stay in the kitchen while you cavorted in the sea with that other woman—uh, that other woman who didn't actually exist.'

'You would have "hated" me?' he asked.

'Of course not. I...I... You...'

Again he got the sense that she had struggled with the urge to say something significant—and then changed her mind.

'I'm very thankful to you for making this day happen. It…it's perfect.'

'I also am grateful that you are here with me,' he replied. 'It is a day I will not forget.'

How could he forget Gemma? He would bookmark this time with her in his mind to revisit it in the lonely, difficult days he would face on his return to Montovia.

A great lump of frustration and regret seemed to choke him as he railed against the fate that had led him to this woman when duty dictated he was not able to follow up on the feelings she aroused in him. When he'd been second in line to the throne, he had protested against the age-old rules governing marriage in Montovia. Now he was crown prince, that avenue had been closed to him.

Not for the first time he wished his brother had not gone up in his helicopter that day.

'Do you want to swim to shore?' she asked. 'C'mon—I'll race you.'

She took off in an elegant but powerful freestyle stroke. Tristan was fit and strong, but he had to make an effort to keep up with her.

They reached the beach with her a few strokes ahead. He followed her as they waded through the shallows to the sand, unable to keep his eyes off her. Her sporty swimsuit showed she meant business when she swam. At the same time it clung to every curve and showcased the smooth expanse of her back, her shapely behind, her slender strong legs.

Gemma Harper was a woman who got even more attractive the better he knew her. *And he wanted her.*

She stopped for him to catch up. Her eyes narrowed. 'I hope you didn't let me win on purpose in some chivalrous gesture?'

'No. You are a fast swimmer. It was a fair race.'

He was very competitive in the sports he played. Being bested by a woman was something new, and he respected her skill. But how could a Montovian, raised in a country where the snow-fed lakes were cold even in midsummer, compete with someone who'd grown up in a beachside city like Sydney?

'I used to race at school—but that was a long time ago. Now I swim for fun and exercise. And relaxation.' She looked at him as if she knew very well that he was not used to being beaten. 'You'd probably beat me at skiing.'

'I'm sure you'd challenge me,' he said. 'Weren't both your parents ski instructors?'

'Yes, but I've only ever skied in Australia and New Zealand. Skiing in Europe is on my wish list—if I ever get enough time away from Party Queens to get there, that is.'

Tristan uttered something non-committal in reply instead of the invitation he wished he could make. There was nothing he would like better than to take her skiing with him. Show her the family chalet, share his favourite runs on his favourite mountains, help her unwind après-ski in front of a seductively warm log fire… But next winter, and the chance of sharing it with Gemma, seemed far, far away.

The sand was warm underfoot as he walked along the beach with her, close enough for their shoulders to nudge against each other occasionally. Her skin was cool and smooth against his and he found it difficult to concentrate on anything but her, difficult to clear his mind of how much he wanted her—and could not have her.

He forced himself to look around him. She'd brought him to an idyllic spot. The vegetation that grew up to the sand was full of birdlife. He saw flashes of multi-coloured parrots as they flew through the trees, heard birdsong he couldn't identify.

'How could you say Sydney is not like living in a resort when a place like this is on your doorstep?' he asked.

'I guess you *would* feel like you were on vacation if you lived around here,' she said. She waved her hand at the southern end of the beach. 'Manly, which seems more like a town than a suburb, is just around the bay. You can hire a two-man kayak there and paddle around to here with a picnic. It would be fun to do that sometime.'

But not with him. He would be far away in Montovia, doing his duty, honouring his family and his country. No longer master of his own life. 'That would be fun,' he echoed. He could not bear the thought of her kayaking to this beach with another man.

She sat down on the sand, hugging her knees to her chest. He sat down next to her, his legs stretched out ahead. The sun was warm on his back, but a slight breeze kept him cool.

'Did you wonder why this beach is called Store Beach?' she asked.

'Not really. But I think you are going to tell me.'

'How did you get to know me so quickly?' she asked, her head tilted to one side in the manner he already found endearing.

'Just observant, I guess,' he said. *And because he was so attracted to her.* He wanted to know every little thing about her.

'There must be a tour guide inside me, fighting to get out,' she joked.

'Set her free to tell me all about the beach,' he said. This sea nymph had bewitched him so thoroughly that sitting on a beach listening to the sound of her voice seemed like heaven.

'If you insist,' she said with a sideways smile. 'Behind us, up top, is an isolation hospital known as the Quarantine Station. Stores for the station were landed here. For the early settlers from Europe it was an arduous trip of many months by sailing ship. By the time some of them got here, they had come down with contagious illnesses like smallpox. They were kept here—away from the rest of Sydney. Some got better...many died.'

Tristan shuddered. 'That's a gruesome topic for a sunny day.'

'The Quarantine Station closed after one hundred and fifty years. They hold ghost tours there at night. I went on one—it was really spooky.'

Her story reminded Tristan of what a very long way away from home he was. Even a straightforward flight was twenty-two hours. Any kind of relationship would be difficult to maintain from this distance—even if it were permitted.

'If I had time I would like to go on the ghost tour, but I fear that will not be possible,' he said.

Had he been here as tourist Tristan Marco, executive of a nebulous company that might or might not produce chocolate, he would have added, *Next time I'll do the ghost tour with you.* But he could not in all fairness talk about 'next time' or 'tomorrow.' Not with a woman to whom he couldn't offer any kind of relationship beyond a no-strings fling because she had not been born into the 'right' type of family.

'We should be heading back to the boat for lunch,' she said. 'I'm looking forward to being a guest for the awesome menu I planned. Swimming always makes me hungry.'

He stood up and offered her his hand to help her. She hesitated, then took it and he pulled her to her feet. She stood very close to him. Tristan took a step to bring her even closer. Her hair was still damp from the sea and fell in tendrils around her face. He smoothed a wayward strand from her cheek and tucked it around her ear. He heard her quick intake of breath at his touch before she went very still.

She looked up at him without saying a word. Laughter danced in her eyes and lifted the corners of her lovely mouth. He kept his hand on her shoulder, and she swayed towards him in what he took as an invitation. There was nothing he wanted more than to kiss her. He could not resist a second longer.

He kissed her—first on her adorable dimples, one after the other, as he had longed to do from the get go. Then on her mouth—her exquisitely sensual mouth that felt as wonderful as it looked, warm and welcoming under his. With a little murmur that sent excitement shooting through him, she parted her lips. He deepened the kiss. She tasted of chocolate and salt and her own sweet taste. Her skin was cool and silky against his, her curves pressed enticingly against his body.

All the time he was kissing her Tristan, knew he was doing so under false pretences. He was not used to deception, had always prided himself on his honesty. He wanted more—wanted more than kisses—from this beautiful woman he held in his arms. But he could not deceive her any longer about who he really was—and what the truth meant to them.

* * *

Tristan was kissing her—seriously kissing her—and it was even more wonderful than Gemma had anticipated. She had wanted him, wanted *this*, from the time she had first seen him in her kitchen. Her heart thudded in double-quick time, and pleasure thrummed through her body.

But she was shocked at how quickly the kiss turned from something tender into something so passionate that it ignited in her an urgent hunger to be closer to him. Close, closer…as close as she could be.

She had never felt this wondrous sense of connection and certainty. That time was somehow standing still. That she was meant to be here with him. That this was the start of something life-changing.

They explored with lips and tongues. Her thoughts, dazed with desire, started to race in a direction she had not let them until now. *Could* there be a tomorrow for her and Tristan? Why had she thought it so impossible? He wasn't flying back to the moon, after all. Long distance could work. Differences could be overcome.

Stray thoughts flew around her brain, barely

coherent, in between the waves of pleasure pulsing through her body.

Tristan gently bit her bottom lip. She let out a little sound of pleasure that was almost a whimper.

He broke away from the kiss, chest heaving as he gasped for breath. She realised he was as shocked as she was at the passion that had erupted between them. Shocked and…and shaken.

Gemma wound her arms around his neck, not wanting him to stop but glad they were on a public beach so that there would be no temptation to sink down on the sand together and go further than kisses. She gave her frantic antennae their marching orders. This. To be with him. It was all she wanted.

'Tristan…' she breathed. 'I feel like I'm in some wonderful dream. I…I don't want this day to end.'

Then she froze as she saw the dismay in his eyes, felt the tension in his body, heard his low groan. She unwound her arms from around his neck, crossed them in front of her chest. She bit her lip to stop her mouth from trembling. Had she totally misread the situation?

'You might not think that when you hear what I have to say to you.' The hoarse words rushed out as if they'd been dammed up inside him and he could not hold on to them any longer.

She couldn't find the words to reply.

'Gemma. We have to talk.'

Did any conversation *ever* go well when it started like that? Why did those four words, grouped together in that way, sound so ominous?

'I'm listening,' she said.

'I have not been completely honest with you.'

Gemma's heart sank to the level of the sand beneath her bare feet. Here it came. He was married. He had a girlfriend back home. Or good old *I'm not looking for commitment.*

Those antennae were now flopped over her forehead, weary and defeated from trying to save her from her own self-defeating behaviour.

She braced herself in readiness.

A pulse throbbed under the smooth olive skin at his temple. 'My family business I told you about…?'

'Yes?' she said, puzzled at the direction he was taking.

'It isn't so much a *business* as such…'

Her stomach clenched. The wealth. The mystery. Her sense that he was being evasive. 'You mean it's a...a criminal enterprise? Like the mafia or—?'

He looked so shocked she would have laughed at his expression if she'd had the slightest inclination to laugh. Or even to smile.

'No. Not that. You've got it completely wrong.'

She swallowed against a suddenly dry throat. 'Are you...are you a spy? From your country's intelligence service? If so, I don't know what you're doing with me. I don't know anything. I—'

The shock on his face told her she'd got that wrong, too.

'No, Gemma, nothing like that.'

He paused, as if gathering the strength to speak, and then his words came out in a rush.

'My family is the royal family of Montovia. My parents are the king and queen.'

CHAPTER NINE

GEMMA FELT AS if all the breath had been knocked out of her by a blow to the chest. She stared at him in total disbelief. 'You're kidding me, right?'

'I'm afraid I am not. King Gerard and Queen Truda of Montovia are my parents.'

'And...and you?'

'I am the crown prince—heir to the throne.'

Gemma felt suddenly light-headed and had to take in a few short, shallow breaths to steady herself. Strangely, she didn't doubt him. Those blue eyes burned with sincerity and a desperate appeal for her to believe him.

'A...a prince? A real-life prince? You?'

That little hint of a bow she'd thought she'd detected previously now manifested itself in a full-on bow to her. A formal bow—from a prince who wore swim shorts and had bare feet covered in sand.

'And...and your family business is—?'

'Ruling the country…as we have done for centuries.'

It fitted. Beyond all belief, it fitted. All the little discrepancies in what he'd said fell into place.

'So…what is a prince doing with a party planner?' Hurt shafted her that she'd been so willingly made a fool of. 'Slumming it?'

Despite all her resolutions, she'd slid back into her old ways. Back at the dating starting gates, she'd bolted straight for the same mistake. She'd fallen for a good-looking man who had lied to her from the beginning about who he was. Lied big-time.

She backed away from him on the sand. Stared at him as if he were a total stranger, her hands balled by her sides. Her disappointment made her want to lash out at him in the most primitive way. But she would not be so uncivilised.

Her voice was cold with suppressed fury, and when she spoke it was as if her words had frozen into shards of ice to stab and wound him. 'You've lied to me from the get go. About who you are— what you are. You lied to get me onto the boat. I don't like liars.'

And she didn't want to hear any more lies.

Frantically, she looked around her. Impenetrable bushland behind her. A long ocean swim to Manly in front of her. And she in a swimsuit and bare feet.

Tristan put out a hand. 'Gemma. I—'

She raised both hands to ward him off. 'Don't touch me,' she spat.

Tristan's face contorted with an emotion she couldn't at first identify. Anger? Anger at *her*?

No—anger at himself.

'Don't say that, Gemma. I…I liked you so much. You did not know who I was. I wanted to get to know you as Tristan, not as Crown Prince Tristan. It was perhaps wrong of me.'

'Isn't honesty one of the customs of your country? Or are princes exempt from telling the truth?'

His jaw clenched. 'Of course not. I'm furious at myself for not telling you the truth earlier. I am truly sorry. But I had to see you again—and I saw no way around it. If you had known the truth, would you have relaxed around me?'

She crossed her arms firmly against her chest. But the sincerity of his words was trickling through her hostility, slowly dripping on the fire of her anger.

'Perhaps not,' said. She would have been freaking out, uncertain of how to behave in front of royalty. As she was now.

'Please. Forgive me. Believe the sincerity of my motives.'

The appeal in his blue eyes seemed genuine. *Or was she kidding herself?* How she wanted to believe him.

'So…no more lies? You promise every word you say to me from now on will be the truth?'

'Yes,' he said.

'Is there any truth in what you've told me about you? About your country? You really *are* a prince?'

'I am Tristan, Crown Prince of Montovia.'

'Prince Tristan…' She slowly breathed out the words, scarcely able to comprehend the truth of it. *Of all the impossible men, she'd had to go and fall for a prince.*

'And everything else you told me?'

'All true.'

'Your brother?'

The pain in his eyes let her know that what he'd told her about his brother's death was only too true.

'Carl was crown prince, heir to the throne, and

he trained for it from the day he was born. I was the second in line.'

'The heir and the spare?' she said.

'As the "spare," I had a lot more freedom to live life the way I wanted to. I rebelled against the rules that governed the way we perform our royal duties. Then everything changed.'

'Because of the accident? You said it's your brother's job you are stepping up to in the "family business," didn't you? The job of becoming the next king?'

'That is correct.'

Gemma put her hands to her temples to try and contain the explosion of thoughts. 'This is surreal. I'm talking to a *prince*, here. A guy who's one day going to be king of a country and have absolute power over the lives of millions people.'

'Not so many millions—we are a small country.'

She put down her hands so she could face him. 'But still… You're a prince. One day you'll be a king.'

'When you put it like that, it sounds surreal to me, too. To be the king was always my brother's role.'

Her thoughts still reeled. 'You don't just live *near* the castle, do you?'

'The castle has been home to the royal family for many hundreds of years.'

'And you probably *own* the town of Montovia—and the chocolate shop with the tea room where you went as a little boy?'

'Yes,' he said. 'It has always been so.'

'What about the chocolate?'

'Every business in Montovia is, strictly speaking, our business. But businesses are, of course, owned by individuals. They pay taxes for the privilege. The chocolate has been made by the same family for many years.'

'Was your little nephew a prince, too?'

'He…little Rudolph…*was* a prince. As son of the crown prince, he was next in line to the throne. He was only two when he died with his mother and father.'

'Truly…truly a tragedy for your family.'

'For our country, too. My brother would have been a fine ruler.'

She shook her head, maintained her distance from him. 'It's a lot to take in. How were you allowed to come to Australia on your own if you're the heir? After what happened to your brother?'

'I insisted that I be allowed this time on my own

before I take up my new duties. Duties that will, once I return, consume my life.'

'You're a very important person,' she said slowly.

'In Montovia, yes.'

'I would have thought you would be surrounded by bodyguards.'

Tristan looked out to sea and pointed to where a small white cruiser was anchored. 'You might not have noticed, but the *Argus* was discreetly followed by that boat. My two Montovian body-guards are on it. My parents insisted on me being under their surveillance twenty-four hours a day while I was in a foreign country.'

'You mean there are two guys there who watch you all the time? Did they see us kissing?' She felt nauseous at the thought of being observed for the entire time—both on the boat and on the beach.

'Most likely. I am so used to eyes being on me I do not think about it.'

'You didn't think you could have trusted me with the truth?'

'I did not know you,' he said simply. 'Now I do.'

Their lives were unimaginably different. Not just their country and their culture. He was *royalty*, for heaven's sake.

'I don't have to call you your royal highness, do I?' She couldn't help the edge to her voice.

'To you I am always Tristan.'

'And my curtsying skills aren't up to scratch.'

Pain tightened his face. 'This is why I went incognito. You are already treating me differently now you know I am a prince. Next thing you'll be backing away from me when you leave the room.'

'Technically we're on a beach, but I get your drift. I'm meant to back away from you across the sand?'

'Not now. But when—' he crossed himself rapidly '—when, God forbid, my father passes and I become king, then—'

'I'd have to walk backwards from your presence.'

'Yes. Only in public, of course.'

'This is…this is kind of incomprehensible.' It was all so unbelievable, and yet she found herself believing it. And no matter how she tried, she could not switch off her attraction to him.

A shadow crossed over his face. 'I know,' he said. 'And…and it gets worse.'

'How can it get worse than having to back away out of the presence of a guy my own age? A guy I've made friends with? Sort of friends—considering I don't generally make pals of people who lie to me.'

'Only "friends", Gemma?' he said, his brows lifted above saddened eyes. 'I think we both know it could be so much more than that.'

Tristan stepped forward to close the gap between them. This time she didn't back away. He traced her face lightly with his fingers, across her cheekbones, down her nose, around her lips. She had the disconcerting feeling he was storing up the sight of her face to remember her.

'Yes,' she admitted. 'I…I think I knew that from the get go.'

It was difficult to speak because of the little shivers of pleasure coursing through her at his touch.

'I did also,' he said. 'I have never felt this way. It was…*instant* for me. That was why I had to see you again—no matter what I had to do to have you with me.'

'I told you I could cast spells,' she said with a shaky smile. 'Seriously, I felt it too. Which is why I resisted you. Whether you're a prince or just a regular guy, I don't trust the "instant" thing.'

'The *coup de foudre*? I did not believe it could happen either—certainly not to me.'

She frowned. 'I'm not sure what you mean?'

'The bolt of lightning. The instant attraction out of nowhere. I have had girlfriends, of course, but never before have I felt this…this intensity so quickly.'

She *had* felt it before—which was why she distrusted it. Why did it feel so different this time?

It was him. *Tristan.* He was quite unlike anyone she had ever met.

She braced her feet in the sand. 'So how does it get worse?'

'First I must apologise, Gemma, for luring you onto the boat.'

'Apologise? There's no need for that. I'm having a wonderful day…enjoying being with you. We could do it again tomorrow—I have vacation days due to me. Or I could take you to see kangaroos…maybe even a koala.'

'You would want that?'

'We could try and make this work.' She tried to tone down the desperation in her voice, but she felt he was slipping away from her. 'We live on different sides of the world—not different planets. Though I'm not so sure about how to handle the prince thing. That's assuming you want to date me?' She laughed—a nervous, shaky laugh that came out as more of a squeak. 'I feel more like Cinderella than ever...'

Her voice trailed away as she read the bleak expression in his eyes. This was not going well.

'Gemma, you are so special to me already. Of course I would like to date you—if it were possible. But before you plan to spend more time with me you need to hear this first,' he said. 'To know why I had no right to trick you. You said you would never hate me, but—'

'So tell me,' she said. 'Rip the sticking plaster off in one go.'

'I am not free to choose my own wife. The heir to the throne of Montovia must marry a woman of noble blood. It is forbidden for him to marry a commoner.'

His words hit her like blows. 'A...a "commoner"? I'm not so sure I like being called a commoner. And we're not talking marriage—we hardly know each other.'

'Gemma, if the way I feel about you was allowed to develop, it would get serious. *Very* serious.'

He spoke with such conviction she could not help but find his words thrilling. The dangerous, impossible kind of thrilling.

'I...I see,' she said. Until now she hadn't thought beyond today. 'I believe it would get serious for me, too.' *If she allowed herself to get involved.*

'But it could not lead to marriage for us. Marriage for a crown prince is not about love. It is about tradition. My brother's death changed everything. Brought with it an urgency to prepare me for the duties that face me. As crown prince I am expected to marry. I must announce my engagement on my thirtieth birthday. A suitable wife has been chosen for me.'

'An arranged marriage? Surely not in this day and age?'

'There is no compulsion for me to marry her. She has been deemed "suitable" if I cannot find an aristocratic wife on my own. And my time is running out.'

Pain seared through her at the thought of him with another woman. But one day together, a few kisses, gave her no claim on him.

'When do you turn thirty?'

'On the eighteenth of June.'

She forced her voice to sound even, impartial. 'Three months. Will you go through with it? Marry a stranger?'

'Gemma, I have been brought up believing that

my first duty is to my country—above my own desires. As second in line to the throne I might have tried to defy it. I even told my family I would not marry if I could not choose my own bride. But as crown prince, stepping into the shoes of my revered brother, who married the daughter of a duke when he was twenty-six and had a son by the time he was twenty-eight, I have no choice but to marry.'

'But not…never…to someone like me…' Her voice trailed away as the full impact of what he was saying hit her. She looked down to where she scuffed the sand with her bare toes. She had humiliated herself by suggesting a long-distance relationship.

Tristan placed a gentle finger under her chin so she had to look up at him. 'I am sorry, Gemma. That is the way it has always been in Montovia. Much as I would wish it otherwise.' His mouth twisted bitterly. 'Until I met you I was prepared to accept my fate with grace. Now it will be that much harder.'

'Aren't princess brides a bit short on the ground these days?'

'To be from an aristocratic family is all that is required—she does not need to be actual royalty. In the past it was about political alliances and dowries...'

Nausea brewed deep in the pit of her stomach. Why hadn't he told her this before he'd kissed her? Before she'd let herself start to spin dreams? Dreams as fragile as her finest meringue and as easily smashed.

Sincere as he appeared now, Tristan had deceived her. She would never have allowed herself to let down her guard if she'd known all this.

Like Alistair, he had presented himself as a person different from what he really was. And she, despite all best intentions, had let down her guard and exposed her heart. Tristan had started something he knew he could not continue with. That had been dishonest and unfair.

She could not let him know how much he had hurt her. Had to carry away from this some remaining shreds of dignity. For all his apologies, for all his blue blood, he was no better than any other man who had lied to her.

'I'm sorry, too, Tristan,' she said. 'I...I also felt the *coupe de foudre*. But it was just...physical.' She shrugged in a show of nonchalance. 'We've done nothing to regret. Just...just a few kisses.'

What were a few kisses to a prince? He probably had gorgeous women by the hundred, lining up in the hope of a kiss from him.

'Those kisses meant something to me, Gemma,' he said, his mouth a tight line.

She could not deny his mouth possessing hers had felt both tender and exciting. But… 'The fact is, we've spent not even a day in each other's company. I'm sure we'll both get over it and just remember a…a lovely time on the harbour.'

The breeze that had teased the drying tendrils of her hair had dropped, and the sun beat down hot on her bare shoulders. Yet she started to shiver.

'We should be getting back to the boat,' she said.

She turned and splashed into the water before he could see the tears of disappointment and loss that threatened. She swam her hardest to get to the boat first, not knowing or caring if Tristan was behind her.

Tristan stood on the shore and watched Gemma swim away from him in a froth of white water, her pale arms slicing through the water, her vigorous kicks making very clear her intention to get as far away from him as quickly as possible.

He picked up a piece of driftwood and threw it into the bush with such force that a flock of parrots soared out of a tree, their raucous cries admonishing him for his lack of control. He cursed loud and long. *He had lost Gemma.*

She was halfway to the boat already. He wished he could cast a wide net into the sea and bring her back to him, but he doubted she wanted more of his deceitful company.

In Montovian mythology, when a cunning hunter tried to capture a water nymph and keep her for himself, he'd drag back his net to find it contained not the beautiful woman he coveted but a huge, angry catfish, with rows of razor-sharp teeth, that would set upon him.

The water nymphs held all the cards.

An hour later Gemma had showered and dressed and was sitting opposite Tristan at the stylishly laid table on the sheltered deck of the *Argus*. She pushed the poached lobster salad around her plate with her fork. Usually she felt ravenous after a swim, but her appetite had completely deserted her.

Tristan was just going through the motions of eating, too. His eyes had dulled to a flat shade of blue, and there were lines of strain around his mouth she hadn't noticed before. All the easy camaraderie between them had disintegrated into stilted politeness.

Yet she couldn't bring herself to be angry with him. He seemed as miserable as she was. Even through the depths of her shock and disappointment she knew he had only deceived her because he'd liked her and wanted her to like him for himself. Neither of them had expected the intensity of feeling that had resulted.

She still found it difficult to get her head around his real identity. For heaven's sake, she was having lunch with a *prince*. A prince from a kingdom still run on medieval rules. He was royalty—she was a commoner. *Deemed not worthy of him.* Gemma had grown up in an egalitarian society. The inequality of it grated. She did not believe herself to be *less*.

She made another attempt to eat, but felt self-conscious as she raised her fork to her mouth. Did Tristan's bodyguards have a long-distance lens trained on her?

She slid her plate away from her, pushed her chair back and got up from the table.

'I'm sorry, Tristan, I can't do this.'

With his impeccable manners, he immediately

got up, too. 'You don't like the food?' he said. But his eyes told her he knew exactly what she meant.

'You. Me. What could have been. What can never be. Remember what I said about the sticking plaster?'

'You don't want to prolong the pain,' he said slowly.

Of course he understood. In spite of their differences in status and language and upbringing, he already *got* her.

This was heartbreaking. He was a real-life Prince Charming who wanted her but couldn't have her—not in any honourable way. And she, as Cinderella, had to return to her place in the kitchen.

'I'm going to ask the skipper to take me to the wharf at Manly and drop me off.'

'How will you get home?'

'Bus. Ferry. Taxi. Please don't worry about me. I'm very good at looking after myself.'

She turned away from him and carried with her the stricken expression on his face to haunt her dreams.

CHAPTER TEN

GEMMA STRUGGLED TO hear what Andie was saying to her over the rise and fall of chatter, the clink of glasses, the odd burst of laughter—the soundtrack to another successful Party Queens function. The Friday night cocktail party at the swish Parkview Hotel was in full swing—the reception being held to mark the official visit of Tristan, crown prince of Montovia, to Sydney.

Gemma had explained to her business partners what had happened on the *Argus* and had excluded herself from any further dealings with him. Tristan had finalised the guest list with Eliza on Thursday.

Tristan's guests included business leaders with connections to the Montovian finance industry, the importers and top retailers of the principality's fine chocolate and cheese, senior politicians—both state and federal—even the governor of the state.

If she didn't have to be here to ensure that the

food service went as it should for such an important function, she wouldn't have attended.

Her antennae twitched. Okay, so she was lying
to herself. How could she resist the chance to see
him again? On a strictly 'look, don't touch' basis.
Because no matter how often she told herself that
she'd had a lucky escape to get out after only
a day, before she got emotionally attached, she
hadn't been able to stop thinking about him.

Not that it had been an issue. Tristan was being
the ideal host and was much in demand from his
guests. He hadn't come anywhere near her, either,
since the initial formal briefing between Party
Queens and its client. She shouldn't have felt hurt,
but she did—a deep, private ache to see that after
all that angst on the *Argus* it seemed he'd been
able to put her behind him so easily.

The secret of his identity was now well and
truly out. There was nothing the media loved
more than the idea of a handsome young European prince visiting Australia. Especially when
he was reported to be 'one of the world's most
eligible bachelors.' She knew there were photog-
raphers swarming outside the hotel to catch the
money shot of Prince Charming.

'What did you say, Andie?' she asked her friend again.

Tall, blonde Andie leaned closer. 'I said you're being very brave. Eliza and I are both proud of you. It must be difficult for you, seeing him like this.'

'Yeah. It is. I'm determined to stay away from him. After all it was only one day—it meant nothing.' One day that had quite possibly been one of the happiest days of her life—until that conversation on Store Beach. 'No big deal, really—unless I make it a big deal.'

'He lied to you. Just remember that,' said Andie.

'But he—' It was on the tip of her tongue to defend Tristan by saying he hadn't out-and-out lied, just skirted around the truth. But it was the same thing. Lying by omission. And she wasn't going to fall back into bad old ways by making excuses for a man who had misled her.

But she couldn't help being aware of Tristan. Just knowing he was here had her on edge. He was on the other side of the room, talking to two older men. He looked every inch the prince in an immaculately tailored tuxedo worn with a blue, gold-edged sash across his chest. Heaven knew what the rows of medals pinned to his shoulder signified—but there were a lot of them. He was the handsome prince from all the fairytales she had loved when she was a kid.

Never had that sense of *other* been stronger.

'Don't worry,' said Andie. 'Eliza and I are going to make darn sure you're never alone with him.'

'Good,' said Gemma, though her craven heart *longed* to be alone with him.

'You didn't do all that work on yourself over six months to throw it away on an impossible crush. What would Dr B think?'

The good thing about having worked on a women's magazine was that the staff had had access to the magazine's agony aunt. Still did. 'Dr B' was a practising clinical psychologist and—pushed along by her friends—Gemma had trooped along to her rooms for a series of consultations. In return for a staff discount, she hadn't minded seeing her heavily disguised questions appearing on the agony aunt's advice page in her new magazine.

Dear Dr B,
I keep falling for love rats who turn out to be not what they said they were—yet I put up with their bad behaviour. How can I break this pattern?

It was Dr B who had helped Gemma identify how her unbalanced relationship with her stepfather had given her an excessive need for approval from men. It was Dr B who had showed her how to develop her own instincts, trust her antennae. And given her coping strategies for when it all got too hard.

'I can deal with this,' she said to Andie. 'You just watch me.'

'While you watch Tristan?'

Gemma started guiltily. 'Is it that obvious? He's just so *gorgeous*, Andie.'

'That he is,' said Andie. 'But he's not for you. If you start to weaken, just think of all that stuff you dug up on the internet about Montovia's Playboy Prince.'

'How could I forget it?'

Gemma sighed. She'd been shocked to the core at discovering his reputation. Yet couldn't reconcile it with the Tristan she knew.

Was she just kidding herself?

She must not slide back into bad old habits. People had warned her about Alistair, but she'd wanted to believe his denials about drugs and other women. Until she'd been proved wrong in the most shockingly painful way.

Andie glanced at her watch. 'I need to call Dominic and check on Hugo,' she said. 'He had a sniffle today and I want to make sure he's okay.'

'As if he *wouldn't* be okay in the care of the world's most doting dad,' Gemma said.

Andie and Dominic's son, Hugo, was fifteen months old now, and the cutest, most endearing little boy. Andie often brought him into the Party Queens office, and Gemma doted on him. One day she wanted a child of her own. She was twenty-eight. That was yet another reason not to waste time on men who were Mr Impossible—or Crown Prince Impossible.

'Where's Eliza?' Andie asked. 'I don't want to leave you by yourself in case that predatory prince swoops on you.'

'No need for name-calling,' said Gemma, though Andie's choice of words made her smile. 'Eliza is over there, talking with the best man at your wedding, Jake Marlowe. He's a good friend of Tristan's.'

'So I believe… Dominic is pleased Jake's in town.'

'From the look of it, I don't know that Eliza would welcome the interruption. She seems to be getting on *very* well with Jake. You go and make your phone call. I'm quite okay here without a minder, I assure you. I'm a big girl.'

Gemma shooed Andie off. She needed to check with the hotel liaison representative about the service at the bar. She thought they could do with another barman on board. For this kind of exclusive party no guest should be left waiting for a drink.

But before she could do so a bodyguard of a different kind materialised by her shoulder. She recognised him immediately as one of the men who had been discreetly shadowing Tristan. She shuddered at the thought that he'd been spying on her and Tristan as they'd kissed on the beach.

'Miss Harper, His Royal Highness the Crown Prince Tristan would like a word with you in the meeting room annexe through that door.' He spoke English, with a coarser version of Tristan's accent.

She looked around. Tristan was nowhere to be seen. From the tone of this burly guy's voice, she didn't dare refuse the request.

Neither did she want to.

Tristan paced the length of the small breakout room and paced back again. Where was Gemma? Would she refuse to see him?

He had noticed her as soon as he'd got to the

hotel. Among a crowd of glittering guests she had stood out in the elegant simplicity of a deep blue fitted dress that emphasised her curves and her creamy skin. Her hair was pulled up and away from her face to tumble to her shoulders at the back. She was lovelier than ever.

He had to see her.

He was taking a risk, stepping away from the party like this. His idyllic period of anonymity was over. He was the crown prince once more, with all the unwanted attention that warranted.

The local press seemed particularly voracious. And who knew if one of his invited guests might be feeding some website or other with gossipy Prince Charming titbits? That was one of the nicknames the media had given him. They would particularly be looking out for any shot of him with a woman. They would then speculate about her and make her life hell. That girl could not be Gemma. She did not deserve that.

And then she was there, just footsteps away from him. Her high heels brought her closer to his level. The guard left discreetly, closing the door behind him and leaving Tristan alone with her. Could lightning strike twice in the same place?

For he felt again that *coup de foudre*—that instant sensation that this was *his woman.*

His heart gave a physical leap at the expression on her face—pure, unmitigated joy at seeing him. For a moment he thought—hoped—she might fling herself into his arms. Where he would gladly welcome her.

Then the shutters came down, and her expression became one of polite, professional interest.

'You wanted to see me? Is it about the canapés? Or the—?'

'I wanted to see you. Alone. Without all the circus around us. I miss you, Gemma. I haven't been able to stop thinking about you.'

Her face softened. 'There isn't a moment since I left the *Argus* that I haven't thought about *you.*'

Those words, uttered in her sweet, melodious voice, were music to his ears.

He took a step towards her, but she put up her hand in a halt sign.

'But nothing has changed, has it? I'm a commoner and you're a prince. Worse, the Playboy Prince, so it appears.'

Her face crumpled, and he saw what an effort it was for her to maintain her composure.

'I...I didn't think you were like that...the way the press portrayed you.'

The Playboy Prince—how he hated that label. Would he ever escape the reputation earned in those few years of rebellion?

'So you've dug up the dirt on me from the internet?' he said gruffly.

She would only have had to type *Playboy Prince* into a search engine and his name would come up with multiple entries.

'Is it true? All the girlfriends? The parties? The racing cars and speedboats?'

There was a catch in her voice that tore at him.

He gritted his teeth. 'Some of it, yes. But don't believe all you read. My prowess with women is greatly exaggerated.'

'You're never photographed twice with the same woman on your arm—princesses, heiresses, movie stars. All beautiful. All glamorous.'

'And none special.'

No one like Gemma.

'Is that true? I...I don't know what to believe.' Her dress was tied with a bow at the waistline, and she was pleating the fabric of its tail without seeming to realise she was doing so.

'I got a lot of attention as a prince. Opportunities for fun were offered, and I took them. There were not the restraints on me that there were on my brother.'

'If I'd been willing, would I have been just another conquest to you? A Sydney fling?'

'No. Never. You are special to me, Gemma.'

'That sounds like something the Playboy Prince might say. As another ploy.'

There was a cynical twist to her mouth he didn't like.

'Not to you, Gemma. Do not underestimate me.'

She was not convinced.

He cursed under his breath. He wanted her to think well of him. Not as some spoiled, privileged young royal. Which he had shown all the signs of being for some time.

'There was a reason for the way I behaved then,' he said. 'I was mad about an English girl I'd met at university. She was my first serious girlfriend. But my parents made it clear they did not approve.'

'Because she was a commoner?'

'Yes. If she'd been from a noble family they would have welcomed her. She was attractive, intelligent, talented. My parents—and the crown advisers—were worried that it might get serious. They couldn't allow that to happen. They spoke to her family. No doubt money changed hands. She transferred to a different university. I was angry and upset. She refused to talk to me. I realised then what it meant to have my choice of life partner restricted by ancient decrees.'

'So you rebelled?'

'Not straight away. I still believed in the greater good of the throne. Then I discovered the truth behind my parents' marriage. The hypocrisy. It was an arranged marriage—my father is older than my mother. He has a long-time mistress. My mother discreetly takes lovers.' He remembered how gutted he'd felt at the discovery.

'What a shock that must have been.'

'These days they live separate lives except for state occasions. And yet they were determined to force me along the same unhappy path—for no reason I could see. I was young and hot-headed. I vowed if I couldn't marry the girl I wanted then I wouldn't marry at all.'

She sagged with obvious relief. 'That's understandable.'

'So you believe me?'

Slowly, she nodded. 'In my heart I didn't want to believe the person I was reading about was the person I had found so different, so...*wonderful*.'

'I was unhappy then. I was totally disillusioned. I looked at the marriages in my family. All were shams. Even my brother's marriage was as cynical an arrangement as any other Montovian royal marriage.'

'And now?'

She looked up at him with those warm brown eyes. Up close he saw they had golden flecks in them.

'It is all about duty. Duty before personal desire. All the heroes in our culture put duty first. They sacrifice love to go to war or to make a strategic marriage. That now is my role. Happiness does not come into the equation for me.'

'What would make you happy, Tristan?'

'Right now? To be alone with my beautiful Party Queen. To be allowed to explore what…what we feel for each other. Like an everyday guy and his girl. That would make me happy.' He shrugged. 'But it cannot be.'

There was no such thing as happiness in marriage for Montovian royalty.

This sea nymph had totally bewitched him. He had not been able to stop thinking about her. Coming up with one scheme after another that would let him have her in his life and explore if she might be the one who would finally make him want to marry—and discarding each as utterly impossible.

'I...I would like that, too,' she said. 'To be with you, I mean.'

He took both her hands in his and pulled her to him. She sighed—he could not tell if it was in relief or surrender—and relaxed against him. He put his arms around her and held her close. She laid her head on his shoulder, and he dropped a kiss on her sweetly scented hair.

Then he released her and stepped back. 'We cannot risk being compromised if someone comes in,' he explained. 'The last thing we want is press speculation.'

'I...I didn't realise that your life was under such scrutiny,' she said.

'That is why I wanted to be incognito. We could not have had that day together otherwise. I do not regret keeping the truth from you, Gemma. I do not regret that day. Although I am sorry if I hurt you.'

She had abandoned the obsessive pleating of the bow on her dress. But her hands fluttered nervously. Looking into her face, he now understood what it meant to say that someone had her heart in her eyes.

She felt it, too. That inexplicable compulsion, that connection. His feelings for Gemma might be the most genuine emotions he had ever experienced. Not *love* at first sight. He didn't believe that could happen so quickly. But something powerful and intense. Something so much more than physical attraction.

'We…we could have another day…together,' she said cautiously, as if she were testing his reaction.

'What do you mean?'

'We could have *two* days. I'm offering you that chance. You don't leave until Monday morning. All day Saturday and Sunday stretch out before us.'

She was tempting him almost beyond endurance. 'You would want us to spend the weekend together knowing it could never be more than that? Not because I don't *want* it to be more, but because it would never be allowed?'

'Yes. I do want that. I…I ache to be with you. I don't want to spend a lifetime regretting that I didn't take a chance to be with you. I keep trying to talk sense to myself—tell myself that I hardly know you; that you're leaving. But at some deep, elemental level I feel I *do* know you.' She shook her head. 'I'm not explaining this very well, am I?'

'I understand you very well—for it is how I also feel. But I do not want to hurt you, Gemma.'

'And I certainly don't want to get hurt,' she said. 'Or hurt *you*, for that matter. But I don't want to be riddled with regret.'

'Remember in three months' time I must announce my engagement to a suitable bride. I cannot even offer to take you as my mistress—that would insult both you and the woman who will become my wife. I will not cheat on her. I will *not* have a marriage like that of my parents.'

'I understand that. Understand and admire you for your honesty and…and moral stance. I'm offering you this time with me, Tristan, with no strings attached. No expectations. Just you and me together. As we will never be allowed to be again.'

He was silent for a moment too long. Common sense, royal protocol—all said he should say no. If the press found out it would be a disaster for her, uncomfortable for him. The Playboy Prince label would be revived. While such a reputation could be laughed off, even admired, for the second or third in line to the throne, it was deeply inappropriate for the crown prince and future king.

Gemma looked up at him. She couldn't mask the longing in her eyes—an emotion Tristan knew must be reflected in his own. Her lovely, lush mouth trembled.

'I should go,' she said in a low, broken voice. 'People will notice we've left the room. There might be talk that the prince is too friendly with the party planner. It…it could get awkward.'

She went to turn away from him.

Everything in Tristan that spoke of duty and denial and loyalty to his country urged him to let her walk away.

But something even stronger urged him not to lose his one chance to be with this woman with whom he felt such a powerful connection. If he didn't say something to stop her, he knew he would never see her again.

He couldn't bear to let her go—no matter the consequences.

Tristan held out his hand to her.

'Stay with me, Gemma,' he said. 'I accept your invitation to spend this time together.'

CHAPTER ELEVEN

NEXT MORNING, in the grey light of dawn, Tristan turned to Gemma, who was at the wheel of her car. 'Where exactly are you taking me?'

'We're heading west to my grandmother's house in the Megalong Valley in the Blue Mountains. She died a few years ago, and she left her cottage to me and my two cousins. We use it as a week-ender and for vacations.'

'Is it private?'

'Utterly private. Just what we want.'

He and Gemma had plotted his escape from the hotel in a furtive whispered conversation the previous night, before they had each left the annexe room separately to mingle with his guests. There had been no further contact with each other until this morning.

While it was still dark, she had driven to his hotel in the city and parked her car a distance away. He had evaded his bodyguards and, with his face covered by a hoodie, had met her without incident. They had both laughed in exhilaration as she'd gunned the engine and then floored the accelerator in a squeal of tyres.

'The valley is secluded and rural—less than two hundred people live there,' Gemma said. 'You might as well be ten hours away from Sydney as two. The cottage itself is on forty acres of garden, pasture and untamed bushland. We can be as secluded as we want to be.'

She glanced quickly at him, and he thrilled at the promise in her eyes. This was a relaxed Gemma, who had pulled down all the barriers she'd put up against him. She was warm, giving— and his without reservation for thirty-six hours.

'Just you and me,' he said, his voice husky.

'Yes,' she said, her voice laced with promise. 'Do you think there's any chance your goons— sorry, your bodyguards—could find us?'

'I was careful. I left my laptop in my suite and I've switched off my smartphone so it can't be tracked. But I did leave a note to tell them I had gone of my own free will on a final vacation and would be back late Sunday night. The last thing we want them to think is that I've been kidnapped and start a search.'

'Is kidnapping an issue for you?' Her grip visibly tightened on the steering wheel.

'It is an issue for anyone with wealth. The royal children are always very well guarded.'

'I'm not putting you at risk, am I? I...I couldn't bear it if I—'

'Here, the risk is minimal. Please do not concern yourself with that. We are more at risk from the media. But I checked that no one was lurking about at my hotel.'

'Can you imagine the headlines if they did find us? *Playboy Prince in Secluded Love Nest with Sydney Party Planner.*'

Tristan rather liked the concept of a love nest. 'They would most likely call you a *sexy* party planner.'

Gemma made a snort of disgust, then laughed. 'I'll own sexy. Or how about: *Playboy Prince Makes Aussie Conquest*? They'll want to get the local angle in, I'm sure.'

'You could also be *Mystery Redhead*?' he suggested.

He found he could joke about the headlines the

press might make about his life—there had been enough of them in the past. Now he was crown prince he did not want to feature in any more. He appreciated the effort Gemma was making to preserve their privacy.

They made up more outrageous headlines as Gemma drove along the freeway until Sydney was behind them.

'Are you going to unleash your inner tour guide and tell me about the Blue Mountains?' Tristan asked as the road started to climb.

'How did you know I was waiting for my cue?' she said.

'Please, go ahead and tell me all I need to know—plus *more* than I need to know,' he said.

'Now that I've been invited...' she said, with a delightful peal of laughter.

Tristan longed to show her Montovia some day—and pushed aside the melancholy thought that that was never likely to happen. He had thirty-six hours with her stretching ahead of him—bonus hours he had not thought possible. He would focus his thoughts on how he could make them special for her.

'They're called the Blue Mountains because

they seem to have a blue haze over them from a distance, caused by the eucalypt oil from the trees,' she said.

'I didn't know that,' he said.

'Don't think of them as mountains like Montovian mountains. Australia is really old, geologically, and the mountains would have been underwater for millions of years. They're quite flat on top but very rugged. There are some charming small towns up there, and it's quite a tourist destination.'

It wasn't that he found what she was saying boring. On the contrary, visiting Australia had long been on his 'to do' list. But Tristan found himself getting drowsy.

For the last three nights he had slept badly, kept awake by thoughts of Gemma and how much he wanted her to be part of his life. Now she was next to him and they were together. Not for long enough, but it was more than he could have dreamed of. For the moment he was content. To drift off to the sound of her voice was a particular kind of joy…

When he awoke, Gemma was skilfully negotiating her car down a series of hairpin bends on a narrow road where the Australian bush grew right to the sides.

'You've woken just in time for our descent into the valley,' she said. 'Hold on—it's quite a twisty ride.'

The road wound through verdant rainforest and huge towering indigenous trees before emerging onto the valley floor. Tristan caught his breath in awe at the sight of a wall of rugged sandstone mountains, tinged red with the morning sun.

'It's magnificent, isn't it?' she said. 'You should see it after heavy rain, when there are waterfalls cascading down.'

The landscape alternated harshness with lush pastures dotted with black and white cattle. There was only the occasional farmhouse.

'Do you wonder why I'm driving so slowly?' Gemma asked.

'Because it's a narrow road?' he ventured.

'Because—ah, here they are. Look!'

A group of kangaroos bounded parallel to the road. Tristan wished he had a camera. His smartphone was switched off, and he didn't dare risk switching it back on.

'You have to be careful in the mornings and evenings not to hit them as they cross the road.'

She braked gently. 'Like that—right in front of the car.'

One after the other the kangaroos jumped over a low spot in the fence and crossed the road. Halfway across, the largest one stopped and looked at him.

'He is as curious about me as I am about him,' Tristan whispered, not wanting to scare the creature. 'I really feel like I am in Australia now.'

'I promised you kangaroos in the wild, and I've delivered,' Gemma said with justifiable triumph.

While he could promise her nothing.

As Gemma showed Tristan around the three-bedroom, one-bathroom cottage, she wondered what he really thought of it. He was, after all, used to living in a castle. The royal castle of Montovia was splendid—as befitted the prosperous principality.

Her internet research had showed her a medieval masterpiece clinging to the side of a mountain and overlooking a huge lake ringed by more snow-topped mountains. Her research had not shown her the private rooms where the family lived, but even if they were only half as extravagant as the public spaces Tristan had grown up in, they would be of almost unimaginable splendour.

And then there was a summer palace, at the other end of the lake. And royal apartments in Paris and Florence.

No doubt wherever he lived, he was waited on hand and foot by servants.

But she would not be intimidated. She was proud of her grandma's house—she and her cousins would probably always call it that, even though it was now their names on the deed of ownership.

She loved how it had been built all those years ago by her grandfather's family, to make the most of the gun-barrel views of the escarpment. To a prince it must seem very humble. But Gemma would never apologise for it.

Tristan stood on the wide deck her grandfather had added to the original cottage. It looked east, to the wall of the escarpment lit by the morning sun, and it was utterly private. No one could see them either from the neighbouring property or from the road.

Tristan put his arm around her to draw her close, and she snuggled in next to him. No more pretence that what they felt was mere friendship. She'd known when she'd invited him to spend his final weekend with her what it would lead to—and it was what she wanted.

Tristan looked at the view for a long time before he spoke. 'It's awe-inspiring to see this ancient landscape all around. And to be able to retreat to this charming house.'

She should have known that Tristan would not look down his princely nose at her beloved cottage.

'I've always loved it here. My grandmother knew what the situation was with my stepfather and made sure I was always welcome whenever I wanted. Sometimes I felt it was more a home than my house in Sydney.'

He turned to look back through the French doors and into the house, with its polished wooden floors and simple furnishings in shades of white.

'Was it like this when your grandmother had it? I think not.'

'Good guess. I loved my grandma, but not so much her taste in decorating. When I inherited with my cousins Jane and John—they're twins— I asked Andie to show us what to do with it to bring it into the twenty-first century. Not only did she suggest stripping it back to the essentials and painting everything we could white, but she used the house as a makeover feature for the magazine. We got lots of free help in return for having the house photographed. We put in a new kitchen and remodelled the bathroom, and now it's just how we want it.'

'The canny Party Queens wave their magic wands again?'

'You could put it like that.'

He pulled her into his arms. 'You're an amazing woman, Gemma Harper. One of many talents.'

'Thank you, Your Highness. And to think we're only just getting to know each other…I have many hidden talents you have yet to discover.'

'I've been keeping *my* talents hidden, too,' he said. 'But for no longer.'

He traced the outline of her mouth with his finger, the light pressure tantalising in its unexpected sensuality. Her mouth swelled under his touch, and she ached for him to kiss her there. Instead he pressed kisses along the line of her jaw and down to the sensitive hollows of her throat. She closed her eyes, the better to appreciate the sensation. How could something so simple ignite such pleasure?

She tilted back her head for more, but he teased

her by planting feather-light kisses on her eyelids, one by one, and then her nose.

'Kiss me properly,' she begged, pressing her aching mouth to his.

He laughed deep in his throat, then deepened the kiss into something harder and infinitely more demanding. She wound her arms around his neck to pull him closer, craving more. Her antennae thrummed softly—not in warning but in approval. She wanted him. She needed him. He was hers. Not forever, she knew that. But for *now*.

This was the first time she had walked into a less-than-ideal relationship with her eyes wide open. It was her choice. With Tristan she had not been coerced or tricked. She just hoped that when the time came she would be able to summon the inner strength to let him go without damage to her heart and soul—and not spend a lifetime in futile longing for him.

But she would not think of that now. Her mind was better occupied with the pleasure of Tristan's mouth, his tongue, his hands skimming her breasts, her hips.

He broke away from the kiss so he could undo the buttons of her shirt. She trembled with pleasure when his fingers touched bare skin. He knew exactly what he was doing, and she thrilled to it.

'I haven't shown you around outside,' she said breathlessly. 'There are horses. I know you like horses. More kangaroos maybe…'

Oh! He'd pulled her shirt open with his teeth. Desire, fierce and insistent, throbbed through her. She slid his T-shirt over his head, gasped her appreciation of his hard, muscular chest.

He tilted her head back to meet his blue eyes, now dark with passion. 'How many times do I have to tell you? The only sight I'm interested in is you. *All of you.*'

CHAPTER TWELVE

THE SUNLIGHT STREAMING through the bedroom window told Gemma she had slept for several hours and that it must be heading towards noon. She reached out her hand to find the bed empty beside her, the sheets cooling.

But his lingering scent on the pillow—on *her*—was proof Tristan had been there with her. So were the delicious aches in her muscles, her body boneless with satisfaction. She stretched out her naked limbs, luxuriating in the memories of their lovemaking. Was it the fact he was a prince or simply because he was the most wonderful man she had ever met that made Tristan such an awesome lover?

She wouldn't question it. Tristan was Tristan, and she had never been gladder that she'd made the impulsive decision to take what she could of him—despite the pain she knew lay ahead when they would have to say goodbye.

Better thirty-six hours with this man than a life-time with someone less perfect for her.

Her tummy rumbled to let her know the hour for breakfast was long past and that she'd had very little to eat the night before.

The aroma of freshly brewed coffee wafted to her nostrils, and she could hear noises coming from the kitchen. She sat up immediately—now fully awake. Tristan must be starving, too. How could she have slept and neglected him? *How could she have wasted precious time with him by sleeping?*

She leapt out of bed and burrowed in the top drawer of the chest of drawers, pulled out a silk wrap patterned with splashes of pink and orange and slipped it on. She'd given the wrap to her grandmother on her last birthday and kept it in memory of her.

She rushed out to the kitchen to find Tristan standing in front of the open fridge, wearing just a pair of blue boxer shorts. Her heart skipped a beat at the sight. Could a man be more perfectly formed?

He saw her and smiled a slow smile. The smile was just for her, and memories of their passion-ate, tender lovemaking came rushing back. The smile told her his memories of her were as happy. They were so good together. He was a generous lover, anticipating her needs, taking her to heights of pleasure she had not dreamed existed. She in turn revelled in pleasing him.

All this she could see in his smile. He opened his arms, and she went straight to them, sighing with pleasure as he pulled her close and slid his hands under the wrap. His chest was warm and hard, and she thrilled at the power of his body. He hadn't shaved, and the overnight growth of his beard was pleasantly rough against her cheek.

For a long moment they stood there, wrapped in each other's arms. She rested her head against his shoulder, felt the steady thud of his heartbeat, breathed in the male scent of him—already so familiar—and knew there was nowhere else she would rather be.

'You should have woken me,' she murmured.

'You looked so peaceful I did not have the heart,' he said. 'After all, you drove all the way here. And I only woke half an hour ago.'

'I…I don't want to waste time sleeping when I could be with you.'

'Which is why I was going to wake you with coffee.'

'A good plan,' she said.

'Hold still,' he said as he wiped under her eye with his finger.

'Panda eyes?' She hadn't removed her mascara the night before in the excitement of planning their escape.

'Just a smear of black,' he said. 'It's good now.'

She found it a curiously intimate gesture—something perhaps only long-time couples did. It was difficult to believe she had only met him on Monday. And would be losing him by the next Monday.

'You've been busy, by the look of it,' she said.

The table was set for a meal. She noticed he had set the forks and spoons face down, as she'd seen in France. The coffee machine hissed steam, and there were coffee mugs on the countertop.

'I hope you don't mind.'

'Of course not. The kitchen is designed for people to help themselves. No one stands on ceremony up here. It's not just me and my cousins who visit. We let friends use it, too.'

'I went outside and picked fresh peaches. The tree is covered in them.'

'You picked tomatoes, too, I see.'

Her grandmother's vegetable garden had been

her pride and joy, and Gemma was determined to keep it going.

'Are you hungry?'

'Yes!'

'We could have breakfast, or we could have lunch. Whatever you choose.'

'Maybe brunch? You're going to *cook*?'

'Don't look so surprised.'

'I didn't imagine a prince could cook—or would even know his way around a kitchen.'

'You forget—this prince spent time in the army, where his title did not earn him any privileges. I also studied at university in England, where I shared a kitchen with other students. I chose not to have my own apartment. I wanted to enjoy the student experience like anyone else.'

'What about doing the dishes?' she teased.

'But of course,' he replied in all seriousness. 'Although I cannot say I enjoy that task.'

She pressed a quick kiss to his mouth—his beautiful, sensual mouth which she had now thoroughly explored. He tasted of fresh, ripe peach. 'Relax. The rule in this kitchen is that whoever cooks doesn't have to do the dishes.'

'That is a good rule,' he said in his formal way.

She could not resist another kiss, and then

squealed when he held her close and turned it into something deeper, bending her back over his arm in dramatic exaggeration. She laughed as he swooped her back upright.

He seemed so blessedly normal. And yet last night he had worn the ceremonial sash and insignia indicating his exalted place in a hereditary monarchy that stretched back hundreds of years. He'd hobnobbed with the highest strata of Sydney society with aplomb. It was mind-blowing.

'The fridge and pantry are well stocked,' she said. 'It's a long way up the mountain if we run out of something.'

'I have already examined them. Would you like scrambled eggs and bacon with tomatoes? And whole-wheat toast?'

'That sounds like a great idea. It makes a pleasant change for someone to cook for me.'

'You deserve to be cherished,' he said with a possessive arm still around her. 'If only—'

'No "if onlys",' she said with a sudden hitch to her voice. 'We'll go crazy if we go there.'

To be cherished by him was an impossible dream…

She was speared by a sudden shaft of jealousy over his arranged bride. Did that well-born woman have any idea how fortunate she was? Or *was* she so fortunate? To be married to a man in a loveless marriage for political expediency might not make for a happy life. As it appeared had been the case for Tristan's parents.

'So—what to do after brunch?' she asked. 'There are horses on the property that we're permitted to ride. Of course they're not of the same calibre as your polo ponies, but—'

'I do not care what we do, so long as I am with you.'

'Perhaps we could save the horses for tomorrow?' she said. 'Why don't we walk down to the river and I'll show you some of my favourite places? We can swim, if you'd like.'

'I didn't pack my swim shorts.'

'There's no need for swimsuits,' she said. 'The river is on our property, and it's completely private.'

A slow smile spread across his face, and her body tingled in response. Swimming at the river this afternoon might be quite the most exciting it had ever been. She decided to pack a picnic to take with them, so they could stay there for as long as they wanted.

* * *

Gemma woke during the night to find Tristan standing by the bedroom window. The only light came from a full moon that sat above the enormous eucalypts that bounded the garden. It seemed every star in the universe twinkled in the dark canopy of the sky.

He was naked, and his body, silvered by the moonlight, looked like a masterpiece carved in marble by a sculptor expert in the depiction of the perfect male form.

Gemma slid out of bed. She was naked, too, and she slid her arms around him from behind, resting her cheek on his back. He might look like silvered marble but he felt warm, and firm, and very much a real man.

'You okay?' she murmured.

He enfolded her hands with his where they rested on his chest.

'I am imagining a different life,' he said, his voice low and husky. 'A life where I am a lawyer, or a businessman working in Sydney. I live in a water-front apartment in Manly with my beautiful party-planner wife.'

She couldn't help an exclamation and was glad he couldn't see her face.

'You know her, of course,' he said, squeezing her hand. 'She and I live a resort life, and she swims every day in the sea. We cross the harbour by ferry to get to work, and I dream of the day I can have my own yacht. On some weekends we come up here, just the two of us, and ride horses together and plan for the day that we...that we—' His voice broke.

He turned to face her. In the dim light of the moon his face was in shadow, but she could see the anguish that contorted his face.

'Gemma, I want it so much.' His voice was hoarse and ragged.

'It...it sounds like a wonderful life,' she said, her own voice less than steady. 'But it's a fantasy. As much a fantasy as that party planner living with you as a princess in a fairytale castle. We... we will only get hurt if we let ourselves imagine it could actually happen.'

'There is...I could abdicate my role as crown prince.'

For a long moment Gemma was too shocked to say anything. 'You say that, but you know you could never step down from your future on the throne. Duty. Honour. Responsibility to the country you love. They're ingrained in you.

You couldn't live with that decision. Besides, I wouldn't let you.'

'Sometimes that responsibility feels like a burden. I was not born to it, like my brother.'

'But you *will* rise to it.'

He cradled her face in his hands, looked deep into her eyes, traced the corner of her mouth with his thumb. 'Gemma, you must know how I feel about you—that I am falling in lo—'

'No.' She put her hand over his mouth to stop him. 'Don't go there,' she said. 'You can't say the *L* word until you can follow it with a proposal. And we know that's not going to happen. Not for us. Not for a prince and a party planner. I...I feel it, too. But I couldn't bear it if we put words to it. It would make our parting so much more painful than...than it's already going to be.'

She reached up and pulled his head down to hers, kissed him with all the passion and feeling she could bring to the kiss. Felt her tears rolling down her cheeks.

'This. This is all we can have.'

Tristan held Gemma close as she slept, her head nestled in his shoulder. He breathed in her sweet scent. Already he felt that even blindfolded he would recognise her by her scent.

His physical connection with this special woman was like nothing he had ever experienced. Their bodies were in sync, as though they had made love for a lifetime. He couldn't label what they shared as *sex*—this was truly making *love*.

Being together all day, cooking companionably—even doing the dishes—had brought a sense of intimacy that was new to him. Was this what a *real* marriage could be like? As opposed to the rigid, hypocritical structure of a royal marriage?

What he felt with Gemma was a heady mix of physical pleasure and simple joy in her company. Was that how marriage should be?

There was no role model for a happy marriage in his family. His parents with their separate lives... His brother's loveless union... And from what he remembered of his grandparents, his grandmother had spent more time on the committees of her charitable organisations than she had with his grandfather. Except, of course, when duty called.

Duty. Why did he have to give up his chance of love for *duty*?

Because he didn't have a choice.

He had never felt for another woman what he felt for Gemma. Doubted he ever would. She was right—for self-protection neither of them could put a label on what they felt for each other—but he knew what it was.

She gave a throaty little murmur as she snuggled closer. He dropped a kiss on her bare shoulder.

The full impact of what he would miss out on, what he had to give up for duty, hit him with the impact of a sledgehammer.

Feeling as he did for Gemma, how could he even contemplate becoming betrothed to another woman in three months' time? He could taste the bitterness in his mouth. Another loveless, miserable royal marriage for Montovia.

He stayed awake for hours, his thoughts on an endless loop that always seemed to end with the Montovian concept of honour—sacrificing love for duty—before he eventually slept.

When Tristan awoke it was to find Gemma dropping little kisses over his face and murmuring that breakfast was ready. He had other ideas, and consequently it was midmorning before they got out of bed.

They rode the horses back down to the river. He

was pleased at how competent Gemma was in the saddle. Despite their differences in social status, they had a lot in common, liked doing the same things, felt comfortable with each other. *If only...*

He felt a desperate urgency as their remaining time together ticked on—a need to landmark each moment. Their last swim. Their last meal together. The last time they'd share those humble domestic duties.

He was used to being brave, to denying his feelings, but he found this to be a kind of torture.

Gemma had *not* been trained in self-denial. But she was brave up until they'd made love for the last time.

'I can't bear knowing we will never be together like this again,' she said, her voice breaking. 'Knowing that I will never actually see you again, except in the pages of a magazine or on a screen.'

She crumpled into sobs, and there was no consoling her. How could he comfort her when he felt as if his heart was being wrenched out of him and pummelled into oblivion?

Tristan tilted her chin up so he could gaze deep into her eyes, reddened from where she'd tried to scrub away her tears. Her lovely mouth trembled.

It was a particular agony to know he was the cause of her pain.

He smoothed her hair, bedraggled and damp with tears, from her face. 'Gemma, I am sorry. I should not have pursued you when I knew this could be the only end for us.'

She cleared her voice of tears. Traced his face with her fingers in a gesture he knew with gut-wrenching certainty was a farewell.

'No. Never say that,' she said. 'I don't regret one moment I've spent with you. I wish it could be different for us. But we went into this with our eyes open. And now…and now I know what it *should* be like between a man and a woman. I had no idea, you see, that it could be like this.'

'Neither did I,' he choked out. Nor what an intolerable burden duty to his beloved country could become.

'So no beating ourselves up,' she said.

But for all her brave words he had to take the wheel of her car and drive back to Sydney. She was too distressed to be safe.

Only too quickly he pulled up the car near his hotel and killed the engine. The unbearable moment of final farewell was upon them.

He gave her the smartphone he had bought to

use in Australia so they could easily stay in touch. 'Keep it charged,' he said.

'I won't use it, you know,' she said, not meeting his eyes. 'We have to make a clean break. I'll go crazy otherwise.'

'If that's what you want,' he said, scarcely able to choke out the words with their stabbing finality. But he stuffed the phone into her bag anyway.

'It's the only way,' she said, her voice muffled as she hid her face against his shoulder. 'But...but I'll never forget you and...and I hope you have a good life.'

All the anger and ambivalence he felt towards his role as heir to the throne threatened to overwhelm him. 'Gemma, I want you to know how much I—'

She pushed him away. 'Just go now, Tristan. Please.'

He wanted to be able to say there could be more for them, but he knew he could not. Instead he pulled the hoodie up over his face, got out of the car and walked back to his life as crown prince without looking back.

CHAPTER THIRTEEN

Ten weeks later

GEMMA SAT ON the bed in a guest room at the grand gated Georgian house belonging to her newly discovered English grandparents. She was a long way from home, here in the countryside near Dorchester, in the county of Dorset in the south-west of England.

In her less-than-steady hand she held the smartphone Tristan had insisted on leaving with her on the last day she'd seen him. It was only afterwards that she'd realised why. If she needed to get in touch with him she doubted the castle staff would put through a call to the crown prince from some unknown Australian girl.

The phone had been charging for the last hour.

She had never used it—rather had kept to her resolve never to contact him. That had not been easy in the sad black weeks that had followed the moment when he had stumbled from her car and had not looked back. But she had congratulated herself on how well she had come through the heartbreak of having her prince in her life for such a short time before she'd had to let him go.

The only time she had broken down was when she had flicked through a gossip magazine to be suddenly confronted by an article about the crown prince of Montovia's upcoming birthday celebrations. It had included photos of Tristan taken at the Sydney reception, looking impossibly handsome. A wave of longing for him had hit her with such intensity she'd doubled over with the pain of it.

Would contacting him now mean tearing the scab off a wound better left to heal?

When she thought about her time with him in Sydney—she refused to think of it as a fling—it had begun to take on the qualities of a fondly remembered dream. After this length of time she might reasonably have expected to start dating again. Only she hadn't.

'Don't go thinking of him as your once-in-a-lifetime love,' Andie had warned.

'I never said he was,' Gemma had retorted. 'Just that he *could* have been if things had been different.'

Now, might she have been given another chance with Tristan?

Gemma put down the phone, then picked it up again. Stared at it as if it might give her the answer. Should she or shouldn't she call him?

She longed to tell Tristan about her meeting with the Cliffords. But would he be interested in what she had to say? Would he want to talk to her after all this time? *Would he even remember her?*

She risked humiliation, that was for sure. By now he might be engaged to some princess or a duchess—that girl in Sydney a distant memory.

But might she always regret it if she didn't share with Tristan the unexpected revelation that had come from her decision to seek out her birth father's family?

Just do it, Gemma.

With trembling fingers she switched on the phone and the screen lit up. So the service was still connected. It was meant to be. She *would* call.

But then she was astounded to find a series of recent missed calls and texts of escalating urgency flashing up on the screen. All from Tristan. All asking her to contact him as soon as possible.

Why?

It made it easy to hit Call rather than have to take the actual step of punching out his number.

He answered almost straightaway. Her heart jolted so hard at the sound of his voice she lost *her* voice. She tried to say hi, but only a strangled gasp came out.

'Gemma? Is that you?'

'Yes,' she finally managed to squeak out.

'Where *are* you?' he demanded, as if it had been hours rather than months since they'd last spoken. 'I've called the Party Queens office. I've called both Andie and Eliza, who will not tell me where you are. Are you at the cottage? Are you okay?'

Gemma closed her eyes, the better to relish the sound of his voice, his accent. 'I'm in Dorset.'

She wondered where he was—in some palatial room in his medieval castle? It was difficult to get her head around the thought.

There was a muffled exclamation in Montovian. 'Dorset, England?'

She nodded. Realised that of course he couldn't see her. 'Yes.'

'So close. And I didn't know. What are you doing there?'

'Staying with my grandparents.'

'They...they are not alive. I don't understand...'

She could almost see his frown in his words.

'My birth father's parents.'

'The Clifford family?'

He'd remembered the name. 'Yes.'

What else did he remember? She hadn't forgotten a moment of their time together. Sometimes she revisited it in dreams. Dreams from which she awoke to an overwhelming sense of loss and yearning for a man she'd believed she would never see again—or hear.

'The people who paid your mother off? But they are not known to you…'

She realised she was gripping the phone so tensely her fingers hurt. 'They are now. I came to find them. After all your talk of your birthright and heritage, I wanted to know about mine. I told my mother I could no longer deny my need to know just because my stepfather felt threatened that she'd been married before.'

Her time with Tristan had made her want to take charge of her life and what was important to her.

'Those people—did they welcome you?'

'It seems I look very much like my father,' she said. In fact her grandmother had nearly fainted when Gemma had introduced herself.

'They were kind?'

The concern in his voice made her think Tristan still felt something for her.

'Very kind. It's a long story. One I'd like to share with you, Tristan.' She held her breath, waiting for his answer.

'I would like to hear it. And there is something important I have to tell you.'

'Is that why you were calling me?'

'Yes. I wanted to fly to Australia to see you.'

'You were going to fly all that way? But it's only two weeks until your birthday party.'

'I want to see you. Can you to come to Montovia?'

For a long moment she was too shocked to reply. 'Well, yes, I would like to see Montovia,' she finally choked out. *Tristan.* She just wanted to see Tristan. Here, there, Australia—she didn't care where. 'When?'

'Tomorrow.'

Excitement or trepidation? Which did she feel more? 'I'll look up flights.'

'I will send a private jet,' he said, without hesitation.

Of course he would.

'And a limousine to pick you up from where you are in Dorset.'

'There's no need. I have a rental car...I can drive—'

'I will send the car.'

When she'd flown to England from Australia she'd had no intention of contacting Tristan. Certainly not of visiting Montovia. The meeting with her grandparents had changed everything.

It wasn't until after she had disconnected the phone that she realised she hadn't asked Tristan what was so important that he'd left all those messages.

The next day the limousine arrived exactly on time and took her to Bristol airport. She was whisked through security and then onto the tarmac.

It wasn't until she began to climb the steps to board the plane that she started to feel nervous. *What the heck was she doing here?*

She'd been determined to take charge of her own life after so many years of acquiescing to men, but then with one word from Tristan—actually, two words: *private* and *jet*—she'd rolled over and gone passive again.

Then he was there, and thoughts of anything else were crowded out of her mind.

Tristan.

He stood at the top of the steps, towering over her. Tall, broad-shouldered, wearing an immaculately tailored business suit in deepest charcoal with a narrow grey tie. His hair was cut much shorter—almost military in style. When she'd last seen him he hadn't shaved for two days and had been wearing blue jeans and a T-shirt. The time before that he'd been wearing nothing at all.

He looked the same, but not the same.

And it was the *not the same* that had her feet seemingly stuck to the steps and her mouth unable to form words of greeting.

He was every bit as handsome as she remembered. But this Tristan appeared older, more serious. A man of wealth and stratospheric status—greeting her on board a private jet that was to fly her to his castle. While she was still very much just Gemma from Sydney.

Gemma looked the same as Tristan had remembered—her hair copper bright, her heart-shaped face pretty, her lovely body discreetly shown off in deep pink trousers and a white jacket. As he watched her, he thought his heart would burst with an explosion of emotion.

He had never lost faith that he would see her
again. That faith had paid off now, after all those
dark hours between the moment he had said goodbye to her in Sydney and this moment, when he
would say hello to her again. Hours during which
he had honoured her request not to contact her.
Hours when he had worked with all the driven
frenzy of the Montovian fisherman searching for
his water nymph to find a way they could be together.

But Gemma stood frozen, as though she were
uncertain whether to step up or back down. There
wasn't a dimple in sight.

Was it fear of flying? Or fear of *him*?

He hadn't said he'd be on the jet to meet her—
he'd had to reschedule two meetings with his father and the inner circle of court advisers to make
the flight. He hadn't wanted to make a promise
he might not have been able to keep. Perhaps she
was too shocked at his presence to speak.

He cursed under his breath. Why hadn't he
thought to radio through to the chauffeur?

Because he'd been too damn excited at the
thought of seeing her so soon to follow through
on detail.

Now he wanted to bound down those steps,

sweep her into his arms and carry her on board. The dazed look in her cinnamon-coloured eyes made him decide to be more circumspect. What had he expected? That she would fall back into his arms when, for all she knew, the situation hadn't changed between them and he still could not offer her anything more than a tryst?

Tristan urged himself to be patient. He took a step down to her, his arms outstretched in welcome. 'Gemma. I can't believe you're in Europe.'

For a long moment she looked up at him, searching his face. He smiled, unable to hide his joy and relief at seeing her again.

At last her lovely mouth tilted upwards and those longed-for dimples flirted once more in her cheeks. Finally she closed the remaining steps between them.

'Tristan. I can't believe it's you. I…I thought I would never see you again. Your smile…it's still the same.'

That puzzled him. Of course his smile was still the same. Probably a lot warmer and wider than any smile on his face since he'd last seen her. But all he could think about was Gemma. Back in his arms where she belonged.

He held her close for a long moment measured by the beating of her heart against him. He breathed in her essence, her scent heart-rendingly familiar.

Gratitude that everything had worked out surged through him. He didn't know how she had come to be just an hour's flight away from him, but he didn't question it. The need to kiss her was too strong—questions and answers could come later.

He dipped his head to claim her mouth. She kissed him back, at first uncertainly and then with enthusiasm.

'Tristan...' she murmured in that throaty, familiar way.

At last. Now everything was going to be as he wanted it.

CHAPTER FOURTEEN

GEMMA HAD ONLY ever seen the inside of a private jet in movies. Was this a taste of the luxury in which Tristan lived? If so, she guessed it was her first look at his life in Montovia. The armchair-like reclining seats, the sofas, the bathrooms... All slick and sleek, in leather, crystal and finest wool upholstery. The royal Montovian coat of arms—an eagle holding a sword in its beak—was embroidered on the fabrics and etched into crystal glasses. No wonder Tristan had not been overly impressed with the *Argus*—it must have seemed everyday to him.

Once they were in the air the attendant, in a uniform that also bore the royal coat of arms, served a light lunch, but Gemma was too tightly wound to eat. Tristan didn't eat much either. She wanted to tell him her news but didn't know how to introduce the topic. They sat in adjoining seats—close, but not intimate. She wasn't yet ready for intimate.

She was grateful when he asked outright. 'So, tell me about your meeting with your new grandparents.'

'They're not new—I mean they've been there all the time, but they didn't know I existed, of course.'

'They honestly had never checked up on your mother over the years?'

The words spilled out of her. 'Their shock at meeting me appeared genuine. The dimples did it, I think; my grandmother has them too. Eliza had joked that the Cliffords would probably want a DNA test, but they scarcely looked at my birth certificate. They loved their son very much. I think they see me as some kind of unexpected gift. And I… Well, I like them a lot.'

'It must have been exciting for you to finally find out about your father,' he said. 'Did it fill a gap for you?'

'A gap I didn't really know was there,' she said. 'You know I had only ever seen one photo of my father? The Cliffordses' house is full of them. He was very handsome. Apparently, he was somewhat of an endearing bad boy, who dropped out of Oxford and was living as a ski bum when he met my mother. His parents were hoping he'd get it out of his system and come back to the fold, but then he…he died. The revelation that he was married came as a huge shock to them.'

'What about the way they treated your mother?'

'I'm not making any excuses for them. I still think it was despicable. But apparently there's some serious money in the family, and there had been gold-diggers after him before. I told them my mother had no idea about any of that. She was clueless about English class distinctions.'

'For your sake, I am glad it's worked out for you…'

Gemma could sense the unspoken question at the end of his sentence. 'But you want to know why I decided to share my adventure with you.'

'Yes,' he said. 'I know you turned on the smartphone I left you because you decided to get in touch with me. I can only suppose it was because of your meeting with your new family.'

'You're right. But before I tell you I want to ask you something.' She felt her cheeks flush warm. 'It's your birthday in two weeks' time. I…I saw in a magazine that you have a big party planned. Are you…are you engaged to be married? To the girl your parents chose for you? Or anyone else?'

'No,' he said, without hesitation.

She could not help her audible sigh of relief.

Tristan met her gaze. 'What about you? Is there another man in your life?'

'There has been no one since…since you.'

'Good,' he said fiercely, his relief also apparent.

Seeing Tristan again told her why she had felt no interest in dating other men. Their attraction was as strong, as compelling, as overwhelming as it had ever been.

'Before I tell you what happened at my grandparents' house, let me say I come to you with no expectations,' she said. 'I realise when it comes down to it we…well, we've only known each other a week, but—'

Tristan made a sound of impatience that definitely involved Montovian cursing. 'A *week*? I feel I have known you a lifetime, Gemma. I know all I need to know about you.'

He planted a swift kiss on her mouth—enough to thrill her and leave her wanting more. She would have liked to turn to him, pull his head back to hers—but not before she'd had her say.

'You might want to know this, as well,' she said. 'You're speaking to a person who is, in the words of her newly discovered grandmother, "very well bred".'

Tristan frowned. 'I'm not sure what you mean.'

It had taken her a while to get her head around what she'd learned. Now she felt confident of reciting the story, but still her words came out in a rush. As if she still didn't quite believe it.

'It seems that on my grandmother's side I am eighth cousin to Prince William, the Duke of Cambridge, through a common distant ancestor, King George II, and also connected by blood to the Danish royal family. One of the connections was "on the wrong side of the blanket", but apparently that doesn't matter as far as genealogy is concerned.'

'But…but this is astonishing.'

She couldn't blame Tristan for his shocked expression; she was sure her grandparents had seen the same look on her face.

'I thought so, too,' she said. 'In fact I couldn't believe it could possibly be true. But they showed me the family tree—to which I am now going to be added, on the short little branch that used to end with my father.'

Tristan shook his head in disbelief. 'After all I have done—'

'What do you mean? What have you done?'

'It is not important,' he said with a slight shake of his head. 'Not now.'

The way he'd said that had made it sound as though it *was* important. She would have to ask him about it at another time. Right now she was more concerned at the impact of her own news.

'I…I wanted to ask you if that connection is strong enough for… Well, strong enough to make things between us not so impossible as when I was just a commoner. Not that I'm not a commoner still, really. But as far as bloodlines are concerned—that's what my grandmother calls them—I…I have more of a pedigree than I could ever have imagined.'

He nodded thoughtfully. 'Forgive me, Gemma. This is a lot to take in.'

A chill ran up her spine. Was she too late? 'I'd hoped it might make a difference to…to us. That is if there *is* an "us".'

His dark brows rose, as if she had said something ridiculous. 'As far as I am concerned there was an "us" from the moment you tried to attack me with that wooden spoon.'

She smiled at the reminder. 'You are never, ever going to let me forget that, are you?'

'Not for the rest of our lives,' he said.

She could see it took an effort for him to keep his voice steady.

'Gemma, I've been utterly miserable without you.'

It was still there between them—she could see it in his eyes, hoped he saw it in hers. The attraction that was so much more than physical. If it no longer had to be denied because of the discovery of her heritage, where might it go from here?

Like champagne bubbles bubbling to the top of a glass, excitement fizzed through her.

'Me...me too. Though I've tried very hard to deny it. Kept congratulating myself on how well I'd got over you. I had no hope, you see. I didn't know—none of us did—that the requisite noble blood was flowing in my veins.'

'Stay with me in Montovia, Gemma. Be my guest of honour at the party. Let me woo you as a prince *can* woo the eighth cousin of a prince of this country.'

Again that word *surreal* flashed through her mind. Perhaps this was all meant to be. Maybe she and Tristan were part of some greater plan. Who knew? And Party Queens could manage without her. She hadn't taken a break since the business had started.

'Yes, Tristan,' she said. 'Show me Montovia. I couldn't think of anything better than spending the next few weeks with you.'

She hugged his intention to 'woo' her—what a delightfully old-fashioned word—to herself like something very precious. Then she wound her arms around his neck and kissed him.

By the time the jet started its descent into Montovia, and the private airfield that served the castle, she and Tristan were more than ready to go further than kisses. She felt they were right back where they'd left off in her grandmother's cottage. He might be a prince, but more than that he was the man she wanted—wanted more than ever.

And they had two weeks together.

She couldn't remember when she'd felt happier.

Gemma caught her breath in admiration as, on Tristan's command to the pilot, the jet swooped low over the town of old Montovia. In the soft light of late afternoon it looked almost too beautiful to be real.

The medieval castle, with its elaborate towers and turrets, clung to the side of a forest-covered mountain with the ancient town nestled below. The town itself was set on the shore of a lake that stretched as far as she could see, to end in the reflections of another snow-capped mountain range. A medieval cathedral dominated the town with its height and grandeur.

'You can see from here how strategically they built the castle, with the mountains behind, the lake in front, the steep winding road, the town walls,' said Tristan, from where he sat beside her. 'The mountains form a natural barricade and fortification—it would be an exceptional army that could scale them. Especially considering there's snow and ice on the passes most months of the year.'

He kept his hand on her shoulder as he showed her what to look for out of the window. Gemma loved the way he seemed to want to reassure himself she was there, with a touch, a quick kiss, a smile. It was like some kind of wonderful dream that she was here with him after those months of misery. And all because she'd followed up on her curiosity about her father.

'It's good to see you taking your turn as tour guide,' she said. 'There's so much I want to know.'

'Happy to oblige,' he said with his charming smile. 'I love Montovia, and I want you to love it, too.'

For just two weeks? She didn't dare let herself think there could be more…

She reached out to smooth his cowlick back into place—that unruly piece of hair that refused to stay put. It was a small imperfection. He was still beautiful in the way of a virile man.

That inner excitement continued to bubble. Not because of castles and lakes and mountains. But because of Tristan. *She loved him*. No longer did she need to deny it—to herself or anyone else. She loved him—and there was no longer any road-block on a possible future together.

'The castle was originally a fortress, built in the eleventh century on the ruins of a Roman *castellum*,' he said. 'It was added to over the centuries to become what it is now. The south extension was built not as a fortress but to showcase the wealth and power of the royal family.'

Gemma laughed. 'You know, I didn't see all that strategy stuff at all. I only saw how beautiful the setting is, how picturesque the town, with those charming old houses built around the square. Even from here I can see all the flower boxes and hanging baskets. Do you realise how enchanting cobbled streets are to Australian eyes?

And it looks like there's a market being held in the town square today.'

'The farmers from the surrounding cantons bring in their goods, and there's other household stuff for sale, too—wooden carvings, metalwork, pottery. We have a beautiful Christmas market in December.'

'I can't wait to see more of the countryside. And to walk around the town. Am I allowed to? Are you? What about your bodyguards?'

'We are as safe as we will ever be in our own town. We come and go freely. Here the royal family are loved, and strangers are rare except for tourists.'

'Do you mean strangers are not welcome?' A tiny pinprick was threatening to leak the happiness from her bubble.

'Are you asking will you be welcome?'

'I might be wondering about it,' she said, quaking a little. 'What will you tell your family about me?'

'They know all about the beautiful girl I met in Sydney. They know I flew to England to get her today. You will be their guest.'

That surprised her. Why would he have told anyone about his interlude with an unsuitable commoner? And wouldn't she be staying with *him*, not his family?

'Will I be seen as an interloper?'

'You are with me—that automatically makes you not a stranger.'

She noticed a new arrogance to Tristan. He was crown prince of this country. Was he really still the Tristan she had fallen for in Sydney? Or someone else altogether?

'I'm glad to hear that,' she said. She paused. 'There's another thing. A girly thing. I'm worried about my clothes. When I left Sydney I didn't pack for a castle. I've only got two day dresses with me. And nothing in the slightest bit formal. I wasn't expecting to travel.' She looked down at what she was wearing. 'Already this white jacket is looking less than its best. What will your parents think of me?'

Being taken home to meet a boyfriend's parents was traumatic at best. When they were a king and queen, the expectation level went off the scale.

'You are beautiful, Gemma. My mother and father are looking forward to meeting you. They will not even notice your clothes. You look fine in what you are wearing.'

Hmm. *They lived in a castle.* She very much

doubted casual clothes would be the order of the day. In Dorset she'd felt totally underdressed even in her newly found grandparents' elegant house. At least she'd managed to pop into Dorchester and buy a dress, simply cut in navy linen.

'I have so many questions. When will I meet your parents? Will...will we be allowed to stay together? Do I—?'

'First, you are invited to dinner tonight, to meet my parents and my sister. Second, you will stay in one of the castle's guest apartments.'

Again there was that imperious tone.

'By myself?'

Her alarm must have shown on her face.

'Don't worry, it is not far from mine.'

'Your apartment?'

'We each have our independent quarters. I am still in the apartment I was given when I turned eighteen. The crown prince's much grander apartment will be mine when its refurbishment is complete. I wanted my new home to be completely different. I could not live there with sad memories of when the rooms were Carl's.'

'Of course...' Her words trailed away.

She shouldn't be surprised that she and Tristan wouldn't be allowed to share a room. Another pinprick pierced that lovely bubble. She hadn't anticipated being left on her own. And she very much feared she would be totally out of her depth.

CHAPTER FIFTEEN

TRISTAN WANTED TO have Gemma to himself for a little longer before he had to introduce her to his family. He also wanted to warn his parents and his sister not to say anything about the work he'd done on what he had privately termed 'Project Water Nymph' in the months since he'd been parted from Gemma.

He sensed in her a reticence he had not expected—he'd been surprised when she'd reminded him she'd only known him for a week. There was no such reticence on his part—he had no doubt that he wanted her in his life. But instinct now told him she might feel pressured if she knew of the efforts he'd gone to in order to instigate change.

Not that he regretted the time he'd spent on the project—it had all been to the good in more ways than one. But news of her noble connections had removed some of that pressure. So long as no one inadvertently said something to her. He wanted her to have more time here before he told her what he'd been doing while she'd been tracking down her English connections.

'Let me show you my favourite part of the castle before I take you to your rooms,' he said. 'It is very old and very simple—not like the rooms where we spend most of our time. I find it peaceful. It is where I go to think.'

'I'd love that,' she said, with what seemed like genuine interest.

'This part of the castle is open to the public in the summer, but not until next month,' he said. 'We will have it to ourselves today.'

He thought she would appreciate the most ancient part of the castle, and he was not disappointed. She exclaimed her amazement at all his favourite places as he led her along the external pathways and stone corridors that hugged the walls of the castle, high above the town.

'This is the remains of the most heavily barricaded fortress,' he explained. 'See the slits in the walls through which arrows were fired? Those arched lookouts came much later.'

Gemma leaned her elbows on the sill of the lookout. 'What a magnificent view across the lake to the mountains! It sounds clichéd, but everywhere I look in your country I see a postcard.'

With her hair burnished by the late-afternoon sun, and framed by the medieval arch, Gemma herself looked like a beautiful picture. To have her here in his home was something he'd thought he'd never see. He wanted to keep her here more than he'd ever wanted anything. This image of Gemma on her first day in Montovia would remain in his mind forever.

He slipped his arms around her from behind. She leaned back against his chest. For a long time they looked at the view in a companionable silence. He was the first to break it. 'To me this has the same kind of natural grandeur as the view from the deck of your grandmother's cottage,' he said.

'You're right,' she said. 'Very different, but awe-inspiring in the same way.'

'I wish we could stay here much longer, but I need to take you to your rooms now so that you can have some time to freshen up before dinner.'

And so that he'd have time to prepare his family for his change in strategy.

If this was a guest apartment, Gemma could only imagine what the royal family's apartments were like. It comprised a suite of elegantly decorated rooms in what she thought was an antique French style. Andie would know exactly how to describe it.

Gemma swallowed hard against a sudden lump in her throat. Andie and Party Queens and Sydney and her everyday life seemed far, far away. She was here purely for Tristan. Without his reassuring presence she felt totally lost and more than a tad terrified. What if she made a fool of herself? It might reflect badly on Tristan, and she *so* didn't want to let him down. She might have been born with noble blood in her veins, but she had been raised as just an ordinary girl in the suburbs.

She remembered the times in Sydney when she had thought about Tristan being *other*. Here, in this grand castle, surrounded by all the trappings of his life, she might as well be on a different planet for all she related to it. Here, *she* was *other*.

A maid had been sent to help her unpack her one pitifully small suitcase. She started to speak to her in Montovian, but at Gemma's lack of response switched to English. The more Gemma heard Montovian spoken, the less comprehensible it seemed. How could she let herself daydream about a future with Tristan in a country where she couldn't even speak the language?

She stood awkwardly by while the maid shook out her hastily packed clothes and woefully minimal toiletries and packed them away in the armoire. Knowing how to deal with servants was totally outside of her experience.

The maid asked Gemma what she wanted to wear to dinner, and when Gemma pointed out the high-street navy dress, she took it away to steam the creases out. By the time Gemma had showered in the superb marble bathroom—thankfully full of luxurious bath products—her dress was back in the bedroom, looking 100 per cent better than it had.

Did you tip the maids? She would have to ask Tristan.

There was so much she needed to ask him, but she didn't want to appear so ignorant he might regret inviting her here.

Her antennae gave a feeble wave, to remind her that Tristan had fallen for her the way she was. He wouldn't expect her to be any different. She would suppress her tremors of terror, watch and learn and ask questions when necessary.

She dressed in the navy sheath dress and the one pair of high-heeled shoes she'd brought with her, a neutral bronze. The outfit had looked fine in an English village, but here it looked drab—the bed was better dressed than she was, with its elegant quilted toile bedcover.

Then she remembered the exquisite pearl necklace her new grandmother had insisted on giving her from her personal jewellery collection. The strand was long, the pearls large and lustrous. It lifted the dress 100 per cent.

As she applied more make-up than she usually would Gemma felt her spirits rise. Darn it, she had royal blood of her own—even if much diluted. She would *not* let herself be intimidated. Despite their own personal problems, the king and queen had raised a wonderful person like Tristan. How could they *not* be nice people?

When Tristan, dressed in a different immaculate dark business suit, came to escort her to dinner, he told her she looked perfect and she more than half believed him.

Feeling more secure with Tristan by her side, Gemma tried not to gawk at the splendour of the family's dining room, with its ornate ceilings and gold trimmings, its finely veined white marble and the crystal chandeliers that hung over the endless dining table. Or at the antique silk-upholstered furniture and priceless china and silver. And these were the private rooms—not the staterooms.

Tristan had grown up with all this as his birthright.

How would she ever fit in? Even though he hadn't actually come out and said it, she knew she was on trial here. Now there was no legal impediment to them having a future together, it was up to her to prove she *could* fit in.

Tristan's parents were seated in an adjoining sitting room in large upholstered chairs—not thrones, thank heaven. His blonde mother, the queen, was attractive and ageless—Gemma suspected some expert work on her face—and was exquisitely groomed. She wore a couture dress and jacket, and outsize diamonds flashed at her ears, throat and wrists. His father had dark greying hair and a moustache, a severe face and was wearing an immaculately tailored dark suit.

Tristan had said they dressed informally for dinner.

Thank heaven she'd changed out of the cotton trousers and the jacket grubby at the cuffs.

Ordinary parents would have risen to greet them. Royal parents obviously did not. Why hadn't Tristan briefed her on what was expected of her? What might be second nature to him was frighteningly alien to her.

Prompted perhaps by some collective memory shared with her noble ancestors, Gemma swept into a deep curtsy and murmured, 'Your Majesties.'

It was the curtsy with which she'd started and ended every ballet class for years when she'd been a kid. She didn't know if it was a suitable curtsy for royalty, but it seemed to do the trick. Tristan beamed, and his mother and father smiled. Gemma almost toppled over in her relief.

'Thank you, my dear,' said his mother as she rose from her chair. 'Welcome.' She had Tristan's blue eyes, faded to a less vivid shade.

The father seemed much less forbidding when he smiled. 'You've come a long way to reach us. Montovia makes you welcome.'

Tristan took her hand in a subtle declaration that they were a couple, but Gemma doubted his parents needed it. She suspected his mother's shrewd gaze missed nothing.

When Tristan's sister joined them—petite, dark-haired Natalia—Gemma sensed she might have a potential friend at the castle.

'Tristan mentioned you might need to buy some

new clothes?' Natalia said. 'I'd love to take you shopping. And of course you'll need something formal for Tristan's party next week.'

Royals no doubt needed to excel at small talk, and any awkwardness was soon dispelled as they sat down at the table. If she hadn't already been in love with Tristan, Gemma would have fallen in love with him all over again as he effortlessly included her in every conversation.

He seemed pleased when she managed a coherent exchange in French with his mother and another in German with his father.

'I needed to fill all my spare time after you left Sydney so I wouldn't mope,' she whispered to him. 'I found some intensive language classes.'

'What do you think about learning Montovian?' he asked.

'I shall have to, won't I?' she said. 'But who will teach me?'

There was a delicious undercurrent running between her and Tristan. She knew why she was here in his country—to see if she would like living in Montovia. But it was a formality, really. If she wanted to be with him, here she would have to stay. Nothing had been declared between them,

so there was still that thrilling element of anticipation—that the best was yet to come.

'*I* will teach you, of course,' he said, bringing
his head very close to hers so their conversation
remained private.

'It seems like a very difficult language. I might
need a lot of attention.'

'If attention is what you need, attention is what
you shall get,' he said in an undertone. 'Just let
me know where I need to focus.'

'I think you might already know where I need
attention,' she said.

'Lessons should start tonight, then,' he said, and
his eyes narrowed in the way she found incredibly sensuous.

'I *do* like lessons from you,' she murmured. 'All
sorts of lessons.'

'I shall come to your room tonight, so we can
start straight away,' he said.

She sat up straighter in her antique brocade dining chair. 'Really?'

'You didn't think I was going to let you stay all
by yourself in this great rattling castle?'

'I did wonder,' she said.

'I have yearned to be alone with you for close on

three months. Protocol might put us in different rooms. That doesn't mean we have to stay there.'

The soup course was served. But Gemma felt so taut with anticipation at the thought of being alone—completely alone—with Tristan she lost her appetite and just pushed the soup around in her bowl.

It was the first of four courses; each course was delicious, if a tad uninspired and on the stodgy side. Gemma wondered who directed the cook, and wondered, if she were to end up staying in Montovia, if she might be able to improve the standard of the menus without treading on any toes.

The thought took her to a sudden realisation— one she had not had time to consider. She knew the only way she would be staying in Montovia was if she and Tristan committed to something permanent.

Finding out the truth about her father's family had precipitated their reunion with such breakneck speed, putting their relationship on a different footing, that she hadn't had time to think about the implications.

If she and Tristan... If she stayed in Montovia she would have to give up Party Queens. In fact

she supposed she would have to give up any concept of having her own life. Though there was
actually no reason why she couldn't be involved
with the business remotely.

She had spent much of the last year working to
be herself—not the version of herself that others
expected her to be. Without her work, without her
friends, without identification with her own na-
tionality, would she be able to cope?

Would being with Tristan be enough?

She needed to talk to Tristan about that.

CHAPTER SIXTEEN

BUT SHE DIDN'T actually have much time alone with Tristan. The next day his parents insisted on taking them to lunch at their mountain chalet, more than an hour and a half's drive away from the castle. The honour was so great there was no way she could suggest she would rather be alone with Tristan.

The chalet was comparatively humble. More like a very large, rustic farmhouse, with gingerbread wood carving and window boxes planted with red geraniums. A hearty meal was served to them by staff dressed in traditional costume—full dirndl skirts for the women and leather shorts and embroidered braces for the men.

'Is this the real Montovia?' she asked Tristan. 'Because if it is, I find it delightful.'

'It is the traditional Montovia,' he said. 'The farmers here still bring their cattle up to these higher pastures in the summer. In winter it is snowed in. People still spend the entire winter in the mountains. Of course, this is a skiing area, and the roads are cleared.'

Would she spend a winter skiing here? Perhaps all her winters?

That evening was taken up with his cousin and his girlfriend joining them for the family dinner. They were very pleasant, but Gemma was surprised at how stilted they were with her. At one point the girlfriend—a doctor about her own age—started to say how grateful she was to Gemma, but her boyfriend cut her off before she could finish the sentence.

Natalia, too, talked about her brother's hard work in changing some rule or another, before being silenced by a glare from Tristan.

And although they all spoke perfect English, in deference to her, there were occasional bursts of rapid Montovian that left Gemma with the distinct impression that she was being left out of something important. It wasn't a feeling she liked.

She tackled Tristan about it when he came to her room that night.

'Tristan, is there something going on I should know about?'

'What do you mean?' he said, but not before a flash of panic tightened his face.

'I mean, Mr Marco, you made a promise not to lie to me.'

'No one is lying. I mean…*I* am not lying.'

'"No one"?' She couldn't keep the hurt and betrayal from her voice.

'I promise you this is not bad, Gemma.'

'Better tell me, then,' she said, leading him over to the elegant chaise longue, all gilt-edged and spindly legged, but surprisingly comfortable.

Tristan sank down next to her. He should have known his family would let the secret slip. No way did he want Gemma to feel excluded—not when the project had been all about including her.

'Have I told you about the myth of the Montovian water nymph?' he asked.

'No, but it sounds intriguing.'

Tristan filled her in on the myth. He told her how he saw her as *his* sea nymph, with her pale limbs and floating hair enticing him in the water of Sydney Harbour.

'When I got back to Montovia, I was like the fisherman who escaped his nymph's deadly embrace but went mad without her and spent his remaining years searching the lake for her.'

Gemma took his hand. 'I was flailing around by myself, too, equally as miserable.'

He dropped a kiss on her sweet mouth. 'This fisherman did not give up easily. I searched the castle archives through royal decrees and declarations to find the origin of the rule that kept us apart. Along the way I found my purpose.'

'I'm not sure what you mean.' she said.

'Remember, I've been rebelling against this rule since my Playboy Prince days? But I began to realise I'd gone about it the wrong way—perhaps a hangover from being the "spare". I'd been waiting for *someone else* to change the rules.'

He gave an unconsciously arrogant toss of his head.

'So I decided *I* was the crown prince. *I* was the lawyer. *I* was the person who was going to bring the royal family of Montovia kicking and screaming into the twenty-first century. All motivated by the fact I wanted the right to choose my own bride, no matter her status or birth.'

'So this was about *me*?'

'Yes. Other royal families allow marriage to commoners. Why not ours?'

'Be careful who you're calling a commoner,'

she said. 'Now I know why I disliked the term so much. My noble blood was protesting.'

Tristan laughed. He loved her gift of lightening up a situation. It would stand her in good stead, living in a society like Montovia's.

'I practically lived in the archives—burrowing down through centuries of documents. My research eventually found that the rule could be changed by royal decree,' he said. 'In other words, it was in the power of the king—my father—to implement a change.'

'You must have been angry he hadn't already done so.'

'I was at first. Then I realised my father genuinely believed he was bound by law. Fact is, he has suffered from its restrictions more than anyone. He has loved his mistress since they were teenagers. She would have been his first choice of bride.'

Gemma slowly shook her head. 'That's so sad. Sad for your father, sad for his mistress and tragic for your mother.'

'It is all that. Until recently I hadn't realised my father's relationship with his mistress stretched back that far. They genuinely love each other. Which made me all the more determined to change the ruling—not just for my sake but for future generations of our family.'

'How did you go about it?'

'I recruited some allies. My sister Natalia who—at the age of twenty-six—has already refused offers of marriage from six eligible, castle-approved suitors.'

'"Suitors". That's such an old-fashioned word,' she mused.

'There is nothing modern about life in the royal castle of Montovia, I can assure you. But things are changing.'

'And you like being that agent of change?'

'I believe my brother would have preserved the old ways. I want to be a different kind of king for my country.'

'That's what you meant by finding your purpose.' She put her hand gently on his cheek, her eyes warm with approval. 'I'm proud of you.'

'Thank you,' he said. 'You met my next recruit tonight—my cousin, who is in love with that lovely doctor he met during their time in the military. Then my mother came on board. She suggested we recruit my father's mistress. It is too late for them, but they want to see change.'

'Your father must have felt outnumbered.'

'Eventually he agreed to give us a fair hearing. We presented a united front. Put forward a considered argument. And we won. The king agreed to issue a new decree.'

'And you did all that—'

'So I could be with my sea nymph.'

For a long, still moment he searched her face, delighted in her slow smile.

'A lesser man might have given up,' she said.

'A lesser man wouldn't have had you to win. If I hadn't met you and been shown a glimpse of what life could be like, I would have given in to what tradition demanded.'

'Instead you came to terms with the role you were forced to step up to, and now Montovia will get a better ruler when the time comes.'

'All that.'

'I wish I'd known what you were doing,' she said.

'To get our hopes up and for them to come to nothing would have been a form of torture. I called you as soon as I got the verdict from the king.'

She frowned. 'What about your arranged bride? Where did she fit into this?'

'I discovered she did not want our marriage any

more than I did. She was being pressured by her ambitious father. He was given sufficient reparation that he will not cause trouble.'

'So why didn't you tell me all this when I told you about my grandparents?'

'I did not want you to feel pressured by what I had done. My feelings for you have been serious from the start. I realised you'd need time to get used to the idea.'

She reached up and put her hand on his face. 'Isn't it already serious between us?'

He took her hand and pressed a kiss into her palm. 'I mean committed. It would be a very different life for you in Montovia. You will have to be sure it is what you want.'

'Yes,' she said slowly.

Tristan felt like the fisherman with his net. He wanted to secure Gemma to live with him in his country. But he knew, like the water nymph, she had to make that decision to swim to shore by herself.

CHAPTER SEVENTEEN

ON FRIDAY MORNING Tristan's sister, Natalia, took Gemma shopping to St Pierre, the city that was the modern financial and administrative capital of Montovia.

Gemma would rather have gone with Tristan, but he had asked Natalia to take her, telling them to charge anything she wanted to the royal family's account. No matter the cost.

St Pierre was an intriguing mix of medieval and modern, but Gemma didn't get a chance to look around.

'You can see the city another time,' Natalia said. 'Montovians dress more formally than you're probably used to. The royal family even more so. You need a whole new wardrobe. Montovians expect a princess to look the part.'

'*You* certainly do,' said Gemma admiringly.

Natalia dressed superbly. Gemma hoped she would be able to help her choose what she needed to fit in and do the right thing by Tristan. She suspected the white jacket might never get an airing again.

Natalia looked at her a little oddly. 'I wasn't talking about me. I was talking about you, when you become crown princess.'

Gemma was too stunned to speak for a moment. 'Me? Crown princess?'

'When you and Tristan marry you will become crown princess. Hadn't you given that a thought?'

Natalia spoke as though it were a done deed that Gemma and Tristan would marry.

'It might sound incredibly stupid of me, but no.'

In the space of just a few days she'd been whisked away by private jet and landed in a life she'd never known existed outside the pages of glossy magazines. She hadn't thought any further than being with the man she loved.

Natalia continued. 'You will become Gemma, crown princess of Montovia—the second highest ranking woman in the land after the queen—and you will have all the privileges and obligations that come with that title.'

Gemma's mouth went suddenly dry and her heart started thudding out of control. How could she, a girl from suburban Sydney, become a princess? She found the thought terrifying.

'It's all happened so incredibly quickly,' she said to Natalia. 'All I've focused on is Tristan—him stepping up to the role of crown prince and making it his own. I…I never thought about what it meant for me.'

Panic seemed to grasp her stomach and squeeze it hard. She took some deep breaths to try and steady herself but felt the blood draining from her face.

Natalia had the same shrewd blue eyes as her mother, the queen. 'Come on, let's get you a coffee before we start shopping. But you need to talk about this to Tristan.'

'Yes…' Gemma said, still dazed by the thought. *They had not talked nearly enough.*

Natalie regarded her from the other side of the table in the cafe she had steered Gemma to. She pushed across a plate of knotted sugar cookies. 'Eat one of these.'

Gemma felt a little better after eating the cookie. It seemed it was a traditional Montovian treat. She must get the recipe…

'The most important thing we've got to get sorted is a show-stopping formal gown for next Saturday night,' said Natalie. 'Tristan's birthday is a real milestone for him. My brother has changed the way royal marriages have worked for centuries so you two can be together. All eyes will be on you. We've got to have you looking the part.'

Again, terror gripped Gemma. But Natalia put a comforting hand on her arm.

'There are many who are thankful to you for being a catalyst for change. Me included.'

'That's reassuring,' said Gemma. Although it wasn't. Not really. What about those who *didn't* welcome change—and blamed her for it?

'The more you look like a princess, the more you'll be treated like one,' said Natalia.

Natalia took her into the kind of boutiques where price tags didn't exist. The clothes she chose for Gemma—from big-name designers, formal, sophisticated—emphasised the impression that she was hurtling headfirst into a life she'd never anticipated and was totally unprepared for.

She had to talk to Tristan.

But by the time she got back to the castle, sat through another formal dinner with his family—this time feeling more confident, in a deceptively simple black lace dress and her pearls—she was utterly exhausted.

She tried to force her eyes to stay open and wait

for Tristan, but she fell fast asleep in the vast antique-style bed before he arrived.

During the night she became aware of him sleeping beside her, with a possessive arm around her waist, but when she woke in the morning he was gone. And she felt groggy and disorientated from a horrible dream.

In it, she had been clad only in the gauzy French bra and panties Natalia had helped her buy. Faceless soldiers had been dragging her towards a huge, grotesquely carved throne while she shouted that she wasn't dressed yet.

CHAPTER EIGHTEEN

BEING CROWN PRINCE brought with it duties Tristan could not escape. He hated leaving Gemma alone for the morning, but the series of business meetings with his father and the Crown's most senior advisers could not be avoided.

Gemma had still been asleep when he'd left her room. He'd watched her as she'd slept, an arm flung over her head to where her bright hair spilled over the pillow. Her lovely mouth had twitched and her eyelids fluttered, and he'd smiled and wondered what she was dreaming about. He'd felt an overwhelming rush of wonder and gratitude that she was there with him.

Like that fisherman, desperately hunting for his water nymph, the dream of being reunited with Gemma was what had kept him going through those months in the gloomy castle archives. He saw the discovery of her noble blood as confirmation by the fates that making her his bride was meant to be.

He'd gently kissed her and reluctantly left the room.

All throughout the first meeting he'd worried about her being on her own but had felt happier after he'd been able to talk to her on the phone. She'd reassured him that she was dying to explore the old town and had asked him for directions to his childhood favourite chocolate shop and tea room. He'd arranged for his driver to take her down and back. They'd confirmed that she'd meet him back at the castle for lunch.

But now it was lunchtime, and she wasn't in the rose garden, where he'd arranged to meet her. She wasn't answering her phone. His driver confirmed that he had brought her back to the castle. Had she gone back to her room for a nap?

He knocked on the door to her guest apartment. No answer. He pushed it open, fully expecting to find her stretched out on the bed. If so, he would revise his plans so that he could join her on the bed and *then* go out to lunch.

But the bed was empty, the apartment still and quiet. There was a lingering trace of her perfume, but no Gemma. *Where was she?*

A wave of guilt washed over him because he didn't know. He shouldn't have left her on her own. He'd grown up in the labyrinth of the castle. But Gemma was totally unfamiliar with it. She might actually have got lost. Be wandering somewhere, terrified. He regretted now that he'd teased her, telling her that some of the rooms were reputed to be haunted.

As he was planning where to start looking for her, a maid came into the room with a pile of fresh towels in her arms. She dipped a curtsy. Asked if he was looking for his Australian guest. She had just seen Miss Harper in the kitchen garden...

Tristan found Gemma standing facing the view of the lake, the well-tended gardens that supplied fruit and vegetables for the castle behind her. Her shoulders were bowed and she presented a picture of defeat and misery.

What the heck was wrong?

'Gemma?' he called. 'Are you okay?'

As he reached her she turned to face him. He gasped. All colour had drained from her face, so that her freckles stood out in stark contrast, her eyes were red rimmed and even her hair seemed to have lost its sheen. She was dressed elegantly, in linen trousers and a silk top, but somehow the look was dishevelled.

He reached out to her but she stepped back and he let his arms fall by his sides. 'What's happened?'

'I...I can't do this, Tristan.' Her voice was thick and broken.

'Can't do what? I don't know what you mean.'

She waved to encompass the castle and its extensive grounds. 'This. The castle. The life. It's so different. It's so *other*.' She paused. 'That's why I came here.' She indicated the vegetable garden, with its orderly plantings. 'Here it is familiar; here I feel at home. I...I pulled a few weeds from those carrots. I hope you don't mind?'

He wasn't exactly sure what she meant by 'other', but her misery at feeling as if she didn't fit in emanated from her, loud and clear.

'I'm sorry, Gemma. I didn't know you were feeling like this. I shouldn't have left you on your own.'

Her chin tilted upwards. 'I don't need a nursemaid, Tristan. I can look after myself.'

'You're in a foreign country, and you need a guide. Like you were *my* guide when I was in your home country.'

She took a deep, shuddering breath. 'I need so much more than a guide to be able to fit in here,' she said. 'I…I was so glad to be here with you—so excited that we could be together when we thought we never could.'

Was so glad?

'Me, too. Nothing has made me happier,' he said.

'But I didn't think about what it would mean to be a *princess*. A princess worthy of you. I'm a Party Queen—not a real queen in waiting. You need more than…than me…for Montovia.'

'Let me be the judge of that,' he said. 'What's brought this on, Gemma? Has someone scared you?'

Who could feel so threatened by the change of order they might have tried to drive her away? When he found who it was, heads would roll.

Gemma sniffed. 'It started with Natalia, she—'

His sister? He was surprised that she would cause trouble. 'I thought you liked her, that she was helping you?'

'I do. She was. But—'

He listened as she recounted what had happened the day before in St Pierre.

'I felt so…ignorant,' Gemma concluded. 'It

hadn't even entered my head that I would be crown princess. And I have no idea of what might be expected of me.'

Mentally, Tristan slammed his hand against the side of his head. Why look for someone to blame when it was himself he should be blaming? He had not prepared her for what was ahead. Because she'd made such a good impression on his family, he had made assumptions he shouldn't have. Once she had swept into that magnificent curtsy, once he had seen the respect with which she interacted with his parents, he'd been guilty of assuming she would be okay.

His gut twisted painfully when he thought about how unhappy she was. And she hadn't felt able to talk to him. The man who loved her.

Tristan spoke through gritted teeth. 'My fault. I should have prepared you. Made it very clear to everyone that—'

'That I'm wearing my princess learner plates?' she said with another sniffle.

He was an intelligent, well-educated man who'd thought he knew this woman. Yet he'd had no idea of what she'd gone through since he'd dumped her into his world and expected her to be able to negotiate it without a map of any kind.

'What else?'

'The maid. I asked her to help me with a few phrases in Montovian, so I could surprise you. She told me her language was so difficult no outsider could ever learn to speak it. Then she rattled off a string of words that of course I didn't understand and had no chance of repeating. I felt... I felt helpless and inadequate. If I can't learn the language, how can I possibly be taken seriously?'

'She loses her job today,' he said, with all the autocracy a crown prince could muster.

Gemma shook her head. 'Don't do that. She was well-meaning. She was the wrong person to ask for help. I should have asked—'

'*Me*. Why didn't you?'

'I...I didn't want to bother you,' she whispered. 'You have so much on your plate with your new role. I...I'm used to being independent.' She looked down at her feet, in their smart new Italian walking shoes.

'I'm sorry, Gemma. I've let you down. I can't tell you how gutted I am that you are so unhappy.'

She looked up at him, but her eyes were guarded. 'I was okay until Natalia mentioned something this morning about when I become queen. She was only talking about the kind of jewellery I'd need, but I freaked. Becoming crown princess is scary enough. But *queen*!'

Now Tristan gritted his teeth. He'd let duty rule him again—to his own personal cost. Those meetings this morning should have been postponed. He might have lost Gemma. Might still lose her if he didn't look after her better. And that would be unendurable.

'Anything else to tell me?'

She twisted the edge of her top between her fingers. 'The old man in the chocolate shop. He—'

'He said something inappropriate?' He found it hard to reconcile that with his memories of the kindly man.

'On the contrary. He told me what a dear little boy you were, and how he was looking forward to treating *our* children when we brought them in for chocolate.'

'And that was a problem?' Tristan was puzzled at the way Gemma had taken offence at those genial words.

'Don't you see? *Children*. We've never talked about children. We haven't talked about our future at all. I feel totally unprepared for all this. All I know is that we want to be together. But is it enough?'

He did not hesitate. 'Yes. I have no doubt of that.'

She paused for so long dread crept its way into his heart.

'I…I'm not sure it is. You can do better than me. And I fear that if I try to be someone I'm not—like I spent so much of my life doing—I will lose myself and no longer be the person you fell in love with. You've grown up in this royal life. It's all so shockingly different for me—and more than a little scary. I don't want to make your life a misery because I'm unhappy. Do you understand that?'

'I will do anything in my power to make you happy.' His voice was gruff.

'I've been thinking maybe your ancestors had it right. When your new spouse comes from the same background and understands your way of life, surely that must be an advantage?'

'No,' he said stiffly. 'Any advantage is outweighed by the massive *dis*advantage of a lack of love in such a marriage.'

'I'm not so sure,' she said. 'Tristan, I need time to think this through.'

Tristan balled his hands into fists. He was not going to beg. She knew how he felt—how certain he had always been about her. But perhaps he had been wrong. After all the royal feathers he had ruffled, the conventions he had overturned, maybe Gemma did not have the strength and courage required to be his wife and a royal princess.

'Of course,' he said.

He bowed stiffly in her direction, turned on his heel and strode away from her.

Gemma watched Tristan walk away with that mix of military bearing and athletic grace she found so attractive. It struck her how resolute he looked, in the set of his shoulders, the strength of his stride.

He was walking out of her life.

Her hand went to her heart at the sudden shaft of pain.

What a massive mistake she had just made.

He must think she didn't care. And that couldn't be further from how she felt.

The truth hit her with a force that left her breathless. This wasn't about her not understanding the conventions of being a princess, being nervous of making the wrong kind of curtsy. It was about her fearing that she wasn't good enough for Tristan. Deep down, she was terrified he would discover her inadequacies and no longer want her. This was all about her being afraid of getting hurt. She had behaved like a spineless wimp. A spineless, *stupid* wimp.

Through all the time she'd shared with Tristan, fragmented as it had been, he had been unequivocal about what he felt for her. He had tricked her onto the *Argus* because he had been so taken with her. He had confessed to a *coup de foudre*. He had left her with his phone because he had wanted to stay in touch. *He had changed the law of his country so they could be together.*

It was *she* who had resisted him from the get go—she who had backed off. *She* who had insisted they break all contact. If he hadn't left those messages on the phone, would she have even found the courage to call him?

And now the man who was truly her once-in-a-lifetime love had left her. He was already out of sight.

She had to catch him—had to explain, had to beg for another chance. To prove to him she would be the best of all possible princesses for him.

But he was already gone.

She ran after him. Became hopelessly confused as she hit one dead end after the other. Clawed against a bolted gate in her frustration. Then she remembered the ancient walkway he had taken her to on that first afternoon. The place where he went to think.

She peered up at the battlement walls. Noted the slits through which his ancestors had shot their arrows. Noticed the steps that wound towards the walkway. And picked up her speed.

He was there. Standing in the same arched lookout where she'd stood, admiring that magnificent view of the lake. His hands were clasped behind his back, and he was very still.

It struck her how solitary he seemed in his dark business suit. How *lonely*. Tristan was considered one of the most eligible young men in the world. Handsome, charming, intelligent and kind. Yet all he wanted was her. And she had let him down.

She swore under her breath, realised she'd picked up a Montovian curse word. And that it hadn't been as quiet as she'd thought.

He whipped around. Unguarded, she saw despair on his face—and an anger he wasn't able to mask. Anger at *her*.

'Gemma. How did you find me here?'

What if he wouldn't forgive her?

'I followed my heart,' she said simply.

Without a word Tristan took the few steps to reach her and folded her in his arms. She burrowed against his chest and shuddered her deep, heartfelt relief. *This was where she belonged.*

Then she pulled back from his arms so she could look up into his face. 'Tristan, I'm so sorry. I panicked. Was afraid I'd let you down. I lost sight of what counts—us being together.'

'You can *learn* to be a princess. All the help you need is here. From me. From my sister…my mother. The people who only wish you happiness.'

'I can see that now. You stepped up to be crown prince. I can step up to be crown princess. *I can do it.* But, Tristan, I love you so much and—'

He put his hand over her mouth to silence her. 'Wait. Don't you remember when we were at your grandmother's cottage? You instructed me not to say the L word until I was able to propose.'

'I do remember.' Even then she'd been putting him off. She felt hot colour flush her cheeks. 'When it comes to proposing, is it within the Montovian royal code of conduct for the woman to do the asking?'

'There's nothing I know of that forbids it,' he said.

'Okay, then,' she said. 'I'll do it. Tristan, would you—?'

'Just because you *can* propose, it doesn't mean I want you to. This proposal is mine.'

'I'm willing to cede proposing rights to you,' she said. She spread out her hands in mock defeat.

He took them both in his, looked down into her face. Her heart turned over at the expression in the blue eyes that had so captivated her from the beginning.

'Gemma, I love you. I love you more than you can imagine. 'Will you be my wife, my princess, my queen? Will you marry me, Gemma?'

'Oh, yes, Tristan. *Yes* to wife. *Yes* to princess. *Yes* to queen. There is nothing I want more than to marry you and love you for the rest of my life.'

Tristan kissed her long and sweetly, and she clung to him. How could she ever have thought she could exist without him?

'There's one more thing,' he said.

He reached into his inner pocket and drew out a small velvet box.

She tilted her head to one side. 'I thought…'

'You thought what?'

'Natalia implied that part of the deal at the crown prince's birthday is that he publicly slips the ring on his betrothed's finger.'

'It has always been the custom. But I'm the

Prince of Change, remember? I *had* intended to follow the traditional way. Now I realise that proposing to you in front of an audience of strangers would be too overwhelming for you—and too impersonal. This is a private moment—*our* moment.'

He opened the box and took out an enormous, multicarat cushion-cut diamond ring. She gasped at its splendour.

'I ordered the ring as soon as my father agreed to change the rule about royals marrying outside the nobility. I never gave up hope that you would wear it.'

He picked up her left hand. She noticed his hand was less than steady as he slid the ring onto her third finger.

'I love you, Gemma Harper—soon to be Gemma, crown princess of Montovia.'

'More importantly, soon to be your wife,' she said.

She held up her hand, twisting and turning it so they could admire how the diamond caught the light.

'It's magnificent, and I shall never take it off,' she said. She paused. 'Natalia said it was customary to propose with the prince's grandmother's ring?'

'That's been the custom, yes,' he said. 'But I wanted to start our own tradition, with a ring that has significance only to us. Your ring. Our life. Our way of ruling the country when the time comes.'

'Already I see how I can take my place by your side.'

'*Playboy Prince Meets His Match*?' he said, his voice husky with happiness.

'*Mystery Redhead Finds Her Once-in-a-Lifetime Love...*' she murmured as she lifted her face for his kiss.

CHAPTER NINETEEN

As GEMMA SWEPT into the castle ballroom on Tristan's arm, she remembered what Natalia had told her. 'The more you look like a princess, the more you'll be treated like one.'

She knew she looked her best. But was it *princess* best?

The exquisite ballgown in shades of palest pink hugged her shape in a tight bodice, then flared out into tiers of filmy skirts bound with pink silk ribbon. Tiny crystals sewn randomly onto the dress gleamed in the light of the magnificent chandeliers under which guests were assembled to celebrate the crown prince's thirtieth birthday.

The dress was the most beautiful she had ever imagined wearing. She loved the way it swished around her as she walked. Where in Sydney would she wear such a gown? Back home she might devise the *menu* for a grand party like this—she certainly wouldn't be the crown prince's guest of honour. What was that old upstairs/downstairs thing? Through her engagement to Tristan—still unofficial—she had been rapidly elevated to the very top stair.

The dress was modest, its bodice topped with sheer silk chiffon and sleeves. Natalia had advised her that a princess of Montovia was expected to dress stylishly yet modestly. She must never attract attention for the wrong reasons, be the focus of critical press or be seen to reflect badly on the throne.

So many rules to remember. Would she ever be able to relax again?

'You are the most beautiful woman in the room,' Tristan murmured in her ear. 'There will be much envy when I announce you as my chosen bride.'

'As long as I'm the most beautiful woman in your eyes,' she murmured back.

'You will always be that,' he said.

The thing was, she believed him. She felt beautiful when she was with him—whether she was wearing a ballgown or an apron.

Yet even knowing she looked like a princess in the glorious gown, with her hair upswept and diamonds borrowed from the queen—*she had borrowed jewellery from a queen!*—she still felt her stomach fall to somewhere near the level of her silver stilettoes when she looked into the room. So many people, so many strange faces, so much priceless jewellery.

So many critical eyes on her.

Would they see her as an interloper?

Immediately Tristan stepped closer. 'You're feeling intimidated, aren't you?'

She swallowed hard against a suddenly dry throat. 'Maybe,' she admitted.

In this glittering room, full of glittering people, she didn't know a soul except for Tristan and his family. And she was hardly on a first-name basis with the king and queen.

'Soon these faces will become familiar,' Tristan said. 'Yes, there are courtiers and officials and friends of my parents. But many of these guests are my personal friends—from school, the military, from university. They are so looking forward to meeting you.'

'That's good to hear,' she said, grateful for his consideration. Still, it was unnerving.

Thank heaven she hadn't been subjected to a formal receiving line. That would come at their formal engagement party, when she'd have the right to stand by Tristan's side as his fiancée. This was supposedly a more informal affair. With everyone wearing ballgowns and diamonds. Did Montovians actually *ever* do informal?

'Let me introduce you to someone I think you will like very much,' Tristan said.

He led her to a tall, thin, grey-haired man and his plump, cheery-faced wife. He introduced the couple as Henry and Anneke Blair.

'Henry was my English tutor,' Tristan said.

'And it was a privilege to teach you, Your Highness,' Henry said.

'Your English is perfect,' said Gemma.

'I was born and bred in Surrey, in the UK,' said Henry, with a smile that did not mock her mistake.

'Until he came to Montovia to climb mountains and fell in love with a local girl,' said his wife. 'Now he speaks perfect Montovian, too.'

Henry beamed down affectionately at his wife. So an outsider *could* fit in.

'Gemma is keen to learn Montovian,' said Tristan. 'We were hoping—'

'That I could tutor your lovely fiancée?' said Henry. He smiled at Gemma—a kind, understanding smile. 'It would be my pleasure.'

'And I would like very much to share with you the customs and history of the Montovian people,' said Anneke. 'Sometimes a woman's point of view is required.'

Gemma felt an immense sense of relief. She couldn't hope to fit in here, to gain the people's respect, if she couldn't speak the language and understand their customs. 'I would like lessons every day, please,' she said. 'I want to be fluent as soon as possible. And to understand the way Montovian society works.'

Tristan's smile told her she had said exactly the right thing.

Tristan had been right, Gemma thought an hour later. Already some of the faces in the crowd of birthday celebration guests were familiar. More importantly, she sensed a swell of goodwill towards her. Even among the older guests—whom she might have expected would want to adhere to the old ways—there was a sense that they cared for Tristan and wanted him to be happy. After so much tragedy in the royal family, it seemed the Montovians were hungry for a story with a happy ending and an excuse for gaiety and celebration.

She stood beside Tristan on a podium as he delivered a charming and witty speech about how he had fallen so hard for an Australian girl, he had worked to have the law changed so they could be together, only to find that she was of noble birth after all.

The audience obviously understood his reference to water nymphs better than she did, judging by the laughter. It was even more widespread when he repeated his speech in Montovian. She vowed that by the time his thirty-first birthday came around she would understand his language enough to participate.

She noticed the king had his head close to a tall, middle-aged woman, chatting to her with that air of familiarity only long-time couples had, and realised she must be his mistress. Elsewhere, the queen looked anxious in the company of a much younger dark-haired man. Even from where she stood, Gemma realised the man had a roving eye.

How many unhappy royal marriages had resulted from the old rules?

Then Tristan angled his body towards her as he spoke. 'It is the custom that if a crown prince of Montovia has not married by the age of thirty he is obliged to announce his engagement on the night of his birthday celebration. In fact, as you know, he is supposed to propose to his future bride in front of his assembled guests. I have once again broken with tradition. To me, marriage is about more than tradition and alliances. It is about love and a shared life and bringing children up out of the spotlight. I felt my future wife deserved to hear me ask for her hand in marriage in private.'

In a daze, Gemma realised she was not the only person in the room to blink away tears. Only now did she realise the full depth of what Tristan had achieved in this conservative society in order to ensure they could spend their lives together.

He took her hand in his and turned them back so they both faced the guests. The chandeliers picked up the facets in her diamond ring so it glinted into tiny shards of rainbow.

'May I present to you, my family and friends, my chosen bride: Gemma Harper-Clifford—future crown princess of Montovia.'

There was wild applause from an audience she suspected were usually rather more staid.

Her fiancé murmured to her. 'And, more importantly, my wife and the companion of my heart.'

'*Crown Prince Makes Future Bride Shed Tears of Joy...*' she whispered back, holding tightly to his hand, wanting never to let it go.

EPILOGUE

Three months later

IF TRISTAN HAD had his way, he would have married Gemma in the side chapel of the cathedral the day after he'd proposed to her.

However, his parents had invoked their roles as king and queen to insist that some traditions were sacrosanct and he would break them at his peril.

His mother had actually made mention of the medieval torture room in the dungeon—still intact and fully operational—should her son imagine he could elope or in any other way evade the grand wedding that was expected of him. And Tristan hadn't been 100 per cent certain she was joking.

A royal wedding on the scale that was planned for the joining in holy matrimony of Tristan, crown prince of Montovia, and Gemma Harper-Clifford, formerly of Sydney, Australia, would usually be expected to be a year in the planning.

Tristan had negotiated with all his diplomatic skills and open chequebook to bring down the planning time to three months.

But he had been so impatient with all the rigmarole required to get a wedding of this scale and calibre off the ground that Gemma had quietly taken it all away from him. She'd proceeded to organise the whole thing with remarkable efficiency and grace.

'I am a Party Queen, remember?' she'd said, flushed with a return of her old confidence. 'This is what I *do*. Only may I say it's a heck of a lot easier when the groom's family own both the cathedral where the service is to take place *and* the castle where the reception is to be held. Not to mention having a limitless budget.'

Now he stood at the high altar of the cathedral, dressed in the full ceremonial military uniform of his Montovian regiment, its deep blue tunic adorned with gold braid and fringed epaulettes. Across his chest he wore the gold-trimmed blue sash of the royal family and the heavy rows of medals and insignia of the crown prince.

Beside him stood his friend Jake Marlowe as his best man, two of his male cousins and an old school friend.

Tristan peered towards the entrance to the cathedral, impatient for a glimpse of his bride. She'd also invoked tradition and moved into his parents' apartment for the final three days before the day of their wedding. He had no idea what her dress—ordered on a trip to Paris she'd made with Natalia—would look like.

Seemed she'd also embraced the tradition of being ten minutes late for the ceremony...

Then he heard the joyous sound of ceremonial trumpets heralding the arrival of the bride, and his heart leapt. He was surprised it didn't set his medals jangling.

A tiny flower girl was the first to skip her way down the seemingly endless aisle, scattering white rose petals along the red carpet. Then Gemma's bridesmaids—his sister, Princess Natalia, Party Queens Andie and Eliza and Gemma's cousin Jane—each in gowns of a different pastel shade, glided down.

The trumpets sounded again, and the huge cathedral organ played the traditional wedding march. At last Gemma, flanked by her mother on one side and her Clifford grandfather on the other—both of whom were going to 'give her away'—started her slow, graceful glide down the aisle towards him.

Tristan didn't see the king and queen in the front pew, nor the hundreds of guests who packed the cathedral, even though the pews were filled with family, friends and invited dignitaries from around the world, right down to the castle servants in the back rows. And the breathtaking flower arrangements might not have existed as far as Tristan was concerned.

All he saw was Gemma.

Her face was covered by a soft, lace-edged veil that fell to her waist at the front and at the back to the floor, to join the elaborate train that stretched for metres behind her, which was attended by six little girls from the cathedral school. Her full-skirted, long-sleeved dress was both magnificent and modest, as was appropriate for a Montovian bride. She wore the diamond tiara worn by all royal brides, and looked every inch the crown princess.

As she got closer he could see her face through the haze of the veil, and he caught his breath at how beautiful she was. Diamonds flashed at her ears—the king and queen's gift to her. And on her wrist was his gift to her—a diamond-studded platinum bracelet, from which hung a tiny platinum version of the wooden spoon she had wielded at their first meeting.

His bride.

The bride he had chosen and changed centuries of tradition for so he could ensure she would become his wife.

Tristan. There he was, waiting for her at the high altar, with the archbishop and the two bishops who would perform the ceremony behind him. She thought her heart would stop when she saw how handsome he looked in his ceremonial uniform. And the love and happiness that made his blue eyes shine bright was for her and only her. It was a particular kind of joy to recognise it.

She had never felt more privileged. Not because she was marrying into a royal family, but because she was joining her life with the man she loved. The *coup de foudre* of love at first sight for the mysterious Mr Marco had had undreamed-of repercussions.

She felt buoyed by goodwill and admiration for the way she was handling her new role in the royal family. And she was surrounded by all the people she loved and who loved her.

There was a gasp from the congregation when she made her vows in fluent Montovian. When Tristan slid the gold band onto her ring finger, and she and the man she adored were pronounced husband and wife, she thought her heart would burst from happiness.

After the service they walked down the aisle as a new royal couple to the joyful pealing of the cathedral bells. They came out onto the top of the steps of the cathedral to a volley of royal cannons being fired—which, Gemma could not help thinking, was something she had never encountered at a wedding before. And might not again until their own children got married.

Below them the town square was packed with thousands of well-wishers, who cheered and threw their hats in the air. *Their subjects.* It might take a while for an egalitarian girl from Australia to truly grasp the fact that she had *subjects*, but Tristan would help her with all the adjustments she would have to make in the years to come. With Tristan by her side, she could face anything.

Tension was building in the crowd below them and in the guests who had spilled out of the cathedral behind them. The first royal kiss of the newly wed prince and his princess was what they wanted.

She looked up at Tristan, saw his beloved face smiling down at her. They kissed.

The crowd erupted, and she was almost blinded by the lights from a multitude of camera flashes. They kissed again, to the almost hysterical delight of the crowd. A third kiss and she was almost deafened by the roar of approval.

Tristan had warned her that lip-readers would be planted in the audience, to see what they might say to each other in this moment. Why not write the headlines for them?

'*Prince Weds Party Planner*?' Tristan whispered.

'*And They Live Happily Ever After...*' she murmured as, together with her husband, she turned to wave to the crowd.

* * * * *

MILLS & BOON®
Large Print – July 2016

The Italian's Ruthless Seduction
Miranda Lee

Awakened by Her Desert Captor
Abby Green

A Forbidden Temptation
Anne Mather

A Vow to Secure His Legacy
Annie West

Carrying the King's Pride
Jennifer Hayward

Bound to the Tuscan Billionaire
Susan Stephens

Required to Wear the Tycoon's Ring
Maggie Cox

The Greek's Ready-Made Wife
Jennifer Faye

Crown Prince's Chosen Bride
Kandy Shepherd

Billionaire, Boss...Bridegroom?
Kate Hardy

Married for Their Miracle Baby
Soraya Lane

MILLS & BOON®
Large Print – August 2016

The Sicilian's Stolen Son
Lynne Graham

Seduced into Her Boss's Service
Cathy Williams

The Billionaire's Defiant Acquisition
Sharon Kendrick

One Night to Wedding Vows
Kim Lawrence

Engaged to Her Ravensdale Enemy
Melanie Milburne

A Diamond Deal with the Greek
Maya Blake

Inherited by Ferranti
Kate Hewitt

The Billionaire's Baby Swap
Rebecca Winters

The Wedding Planner's Big Day
Cara Colter

Holiday with the Best Man
Kate Hardy

Tempted by Her Tycoon Boss
Jennie Adams

0716 Rom LP